lt

y

t Peter Hunter ist ein alter Hase im Geschäft. Ob im In- oder nd, wann immer es gilt, das Verbrechen zu bekämpfen – Hun- zur Stelle und riskiert Leib und Leben. Unter seinen Kolle- eim Britischen Geheimdienst gilt er als Einzelgänger. Der bei seinen Operationen gibt ihm Recht, auch wenn Hunter haarscharf dem Tod entrinnt.

n seine neue Chefin in der Londoner Zentrale unerwartet in nendienst abkommandiert und ihm zudem den völlig unfähi- ssistenten Percy Horn zur Seite stellt, versteht Hunter die nicht mehr. Die Schreibtischjobs, die ihm aufgebürdet wer- ermürben den versierten Agenten. Doch unversehens stößt er er Akte auf eine grausige Spur: Ein blutiges Geheimnis aus rgangenheit ...

at damals Frau und Kind eines Kollegen umgebracht? Was höchste Geheimdienststellen mit den grausigen Morden zu Varum sterben erneut Menschen?

r und sein Assistent Percy befinden sich plötzlich in einem gefährlichen Netz aus Korruption und politischen Intrigen. ie Maschen werden immer enger gezogen ...

Lernthriller Englisch

SCHATTEN DER VERGANGENHEIT

Story: Susi Weichselbaumer
Übersetzung: Naomi Salisbury

Compact Verlag

Bisher sind in dieser Reihe erschienen:
- Compact Lernthriller Englisch: Grundwortschatz, Aufbauwortschatz, Grammatik, Konversation

In der Reihe Lernkrimi sind erschienen:
- Compact Lernkrimi Englisch: Grundwortschatz, Aufbauwortschatz, Grammatik, Konversation
- Compact Lernkrimi Englisch GB/US: Grammatik, Konversation
- Compact Lernkrimi Business English: Wortschatz, Konversation
- Compact Lernkrimi Französisch: Grundwortschatz, Aufbauwortschatz, Grammatik, Konversation
- Compact Lernkrimi Italienisch: Grundwortschatz, Aufbauwortschatz, Grammatik, Konversation
- Compact Lernkrimi Spanisch: Grundwortschatz, Aufbauwortschatz, Grammatik, Konversation
- Compact Lernkrimi Deutsch: Grundwortschatz, Grammatik

In der Reihe Schüler-Lernkrimi sind erschienen:
- Compact Schüler-Lernkrimi Englisch
- Compact Schüler-Lernkrimi Französisch
- Compact Schüler-Lernkrimi Spanisch
- Compact Schüler-Lernkrimi Latein
- Compact Schüler-Lernkrimi Deutsch: Grammatik, Aufsatz
- Compact Schüler-Lernkrimi Mathematik

In der Reihe Lernstory Mystery sind erschienen:
- Compact Lernstory Mystery Englisch: Grundwortschatz, Aufbauwortschatz

Weitere Titel sind in Vorbereitung.

Chefredaktion: Dr. Angela Sendlinger
Redaktion: Grit Sperlich
Fachredaktion: Autumn Pierce
Produktion: Wolfram Friedrich
Titelillustration: Karl Knospe
Typographischer Entwurf: Maria Seidel
Umschlaggestaltung: Carsten Abelbeck

ISBN-13: 978-3-8174-7570-4
ISBN-10: 3-8174-7570-5
7275705

Besuchen Sie uns im Internet: www.compactverlag.de

Vorwort

Mit dem neuen, spannenden Compact Lernthril
Englischkenntnisse auf schnelle und einfach
auffrischen und überprüfen.
Agent Hunter erleichtert das Sprachtrainin
Humor. Er und seine mysteriösen Fälle stehen i
zusammenhängenden Story.
Der Thriller wird auf jeder Seite durch abwe
kurzweilige Übungen ergänzt, die das Lerne
spannend machen.
Prüfen Sie Ihr Englisch in Lückentexten, Zuo
setzungsaufgaben, in Buchstabenspielen und K
Ob im Bus oder in der Bahn, im Wartezimme
der Mittagspause – das Sprachtraining im hand
die ideale Trainingsmöglichkeit für zwischend
Schreiben Sie die Lösungen einfach ins Buch!
Die richtigen Antworten sind in einem eigenen
mengefasst.

Und nun kann die Spannung beginnen …

Viel Spaß und Erfolg!

Die Ereignisse und die handelnden Personen in diesem
Etwaige Ähnlichkeiten mit tatsächlichen Ereignissen
wären rein zufällig und unbeabsichtigt.

Inh

Lern
Abs
Lösu

Sto

Age
Ausl
ter is
gen
Erfo
oft n

Als i
den
gen
Welt
den,
in ei
der V
Wer
habe
tun?
Hunt
lebe
Und

Shadows of the past

“My hero! Give it to the bad boys!” Cindy held Mike tightly by the lapels of his black winter jacket. She fixed him with an exaggeratedly strict look and spoke in a low, pathetic tone.
“Yes, boss,” nodded her husband eagerly. He immediately grinned, his eyes gleaming and mischievous, “But only if you give me a kiss first for strength. I’m very weak.”
“And what do I get for that?” countered Cindy.
“Well, if it’s like that, then ...” Before Mike could finish the sentence he felt her warm lips against his. During the kiss, he couldn’t prevent himself from beginning to smile again, and Cindy punished him by sucking hard on his top lip.

Übung 1: Finden Sie die richtigen Antworten auf die unten stehenden Fragen!

1. What is your name?
   a) ☐ My name is Mike.
   b) ☐ You call me Mike.

2. Where do you live?
   a) ☐ I am living in London.
   b) ☐ I live in London.

3. Are you married?
   a) ☐ Yes, I am married.
   b) ☐ Yes, I am being married.

4. Where do you work?

a) ☐ I work by the Secret Service.

b) ☐ I work for the Secret Service.

5. Is your job dangerous?

a) ☐ Yes, there is always dangerous.

b) ☐ Yes, there is always danger.

6. Do you have a family?

a) ☐ Yes, I am having a family.

b) ☐ Yes, I have a family.

In the meantime, Michelle had obviously grown bored. She yanked at her mother's trousers and dug her little finger into the seam of her trouser pocket. She could just reach that high. Then she tugged once, very hard. Her parents gave up the kissing ritual. Her father beamed down at his young daughter proudly and bent down: "Michelle, sweetheart, would you like a little kiss like your Mummy?"

"No, I'm four," answered the child and shook her short, dark curls to confirm her objection. Actually, she was only three years old, but every time she tried to say "three", one of her parents corrected her repeating the number to her loudly and clearly. With "four" this did not happen; therefore, she was four.

Cindy let the door lock itself behind Mike and took Michelle in her arms. "Captain, full speed ahead to the bath!" The brown curls flew as the girl nodded joyfully. The bath was better than the beach. There was always sand on the beach between her toes and teeth and the seawater was far too cold.

Übung 2: Finden Sie das passende Gegenteil im Text!

1. lenient ________________________
2. strong ________________________
3. interested ________________________
4. indistinctly ________________________
5. quietly ________________________
6. worse ________________________

Übung 3: Setzen Sie die Verben in die richtige Zeitform!

While she (1. soap) ________ the little girl's back, Cindy's thoughts (2. begin) _______ to wander. It (3. be) ________ like this every time she had been on holiday with Mike. As it was, they (4. have) ________ ten days at the most and every day a phone call (5. come) _________ from the Head Office.

Every time Mike (6. order) _________ somewhere for a last minute operation. Once they (7. even have) ________________ to break off a ski holiday in Austria in the middle of the piste. Since then, they (8. always come) _______________ to this summerhouse on the coast of Cornwall.

From there it wasn't so far to Secret Service Headquarters in London. Funnily enough, earlier she had thought the life of a secret agent's wife would be thrilling, exciting, dangerous and wildly romantic. Now here she was sitting in a typical, whitewashed summerhouse with blue-striped shutters and a view over the cliffs; the path to the beach winding its way between them. Her family and friends considered her bourgeois and didn't even let her speak about it. They thought Mike worked at the London tax office. "The Secret Service couldn't have given him a stupider alias," she said out loud.

"Stoopid alis!" shrieked Michelle and hit the mountain of foam in front of her with her tiny fists. Water sprayed out of the tub on to her mother's blouse and trousers.

"Michelle!" she cried, as she slowly raised herself from a crouching position.

With her right hand she leaned on the edge of the bath. With her left she pulled the material of her blouse away from her stomach, where it lay cold and clammy. The draught, which streamed in through the open bathroom door, made her shiver in her wet things.

ÜBUNG 4 !

Übung 4: Beantworten Sie die Fragen zum Text!

1. Where is the family at the beginning of the story?

____

2. Why does Michelle insist she is four years old?

____

3. Why are the family holidays often disturbed?

____

4. What attracted Cindy to being a secret agent's wife?

____

5. How does Cindy get so wet?

____

An arm wrapped round her neck.

Übung 5: Welche Wörter gehören in die Lücken?
(splash, dry, foam, wet, bathtub, moist)

"Mike, I'm sopping wet 1. ____________________," she began and tried to wriggle out of his grasp. The arm held her tightly. Slowly, the pressure on her throat became stronger.

"Mike …" she repeated.

"Oh boy!" cheered Michelle and hit the water again.

There was a muffled 2. ________________ as she hit the surface of the water rather than the sparse remains of the foam mountain. A loud bang rang out through the 3. __________________________ humidity of the bathroom. The sound echoed against the tiles. The bathroom fell silent. Red-coloured threads wound their way through the milky water and collided with pieces of 4. ______________________.

Tearing herself free of the grasp with all her strength, Cindy threw herself towards the bathtub, screaming. A second shot caught her directly in the back. Her knees gave way and she sank down on her haunches in front of the 5. ________________. She stretched both hands out towards Michelle and covered the little girl, keeping the dark, shiny curls 6. ________________.

ÜBUNG 6 !

Übung 6: Setzen Sie die richtigen Pronomen in die Lücken ein!

Agent Peter Hunter heaved a cardboard box along the corridor. To 1. ________ disappointment 2. ________ had recently received notice that 3. ________ was being moved from external duties to internal duties and must change to office work.

4. ________ arms were slowly becoming stiff. Apart from that, the edges of the box were cutting into the palms of 5. ______ hands and 6. ________ could hardly see anything.

Jutting out of the box were a folder and a trophy with a silver ball on the lid, half covered by a blue and yellow-striped scarf. He had got 7. ________ in his last year at school. Back then, there was hardly a Chelsea home game that he and 8. __________ mates didn't attend.

"Excuse me, I don't want that", a young voice apologised. Someone had bumped into him head-on. Glancing sideways Hunter recognised Waldner hurrying past him.
Or was the lad called Wildner? These young agents all looked the same: Black designer suit, Italian designer shoes; polished till they shone, sunglasses; which they never took off their noses even in the office. Recently new recruits from the Academy were just no use.
At 45, Peter Hunter was an "old hand" in the business. He had successfully led international and national operations. Under orders from the English Secret Service, he had journeyed into the deepest jungle and swum half a sea – in short: he had undertaken every adventurous mission.
All right, the episode with the pedalo had brought him the usual jokes from his colleagues. He had, in fact, nabbed some escaping criminals after a good two-hour chase on a lake, but for a week afterwards could hardly move due to aching muscles.

Übung 7: Um welches Kleidungsstück oder Material handelt es sich bei den Beschreibungen?

1. A smart, matching set of jacket and trousers or skirt:

___

2. Worn on the beach or at the swimming pool:

___

3. Protect the eyes from strong sunlight:

___

4. The end of a jacket or shirt sleeve:

____

5. Synonym for a dress:

____

6. Has ribs, or 'stripes' and is often used for trousers:

____

7. What the arm is contained in:

____

8. Stretches to fit whoever is wearing it:

____

"Don't give yourself lumbago, Hunter," Stuart teased him while the agent stepped out of the lift and scrutinised Hunter mockingly. Hunter stood casually next to the lift door on one leg. With the other leg bent he leant against the wall. He balanced his box on his thigh while trying in vain to reach the lift button with his free hand.

"Well, if it certainly looks like a removal man." The young man in his made-to-measure suit stayed where he was. Still blocking the lift door, he turned away:
"Are you really going and making room for the rest of us or are you staying on to supervise the next generation in both word and deed?"
"Stuart, my dear, we'll talk about it later when you can grow a beard and not just bumfluff."
Hunter swivelled around on the leg he was standing on and gripped

the box tightly again with both hands. Stuart moved out of the way, annoyed.

Übung 8: Wie lautet der Komparativ?

1. My new job will be much _______________ (quiet).

2. Stuart thinks he is _______________ (smart) than Hunter.

3. The box was getting _____________ (heavy) by the minute.

4. The lift button was _________________________ (far) away than Hunter thought.

5. Are you ______________ (old) than the other agents?

6. I think the younger agents are _____________ (bad) than the older ones.

The lift door shut with a hiss behind Hunter.
"Seven." He murmured from behind his box.
"You've got your hands full there," remarked a raw, but warm and pleasant voice. An arm slid past him and he saw long, slim fingers as they pressed the button next to number seven. Then the arm returned into an expensive, dark-blue suit jacket. Between the corner of the folder and the trophy with the silver ball Hunter stole a glance at his fellow traveller.
He could only catch a glimpse at a side angle, but what he saw was quite something.
"Hey!" he thought. Shapely legs in pumps which were perhaps too high – he estimated the woman to be a good 1.70 m in her stocking

feet. The skirt of her severely cut suit ended just below the knee. One small movement and the hem would slide even higher. The trophy blocked his view of the rest of her. His impression continued again from her hair. This artistic construction had a curious rigidity. She had definitely added a lot of effort and hairspray. He grinned and thought, "But would it look the same if she could put on a motorcycle helmet? With those legs …"

Übung 9: Welche Antwort passt?

1. Hi there, how are you?
   a) ☐ How do you do?
   b) ☐ I'm fine, thanks and you?
   c) ☐ Great let's meet there!

2.What do you do here?
   a) ☐ I'm standing in the lift.
   b) ☐ I'm a secret agent.
   c) ☐ I'm not normally here.

3. Have you worked here long?
   a) ☐ I've been in since 8am this morning.
   b) ☐ No, I don't plan to stay.
   c) ☐ No, I've only been here a few months.

4. Do you like it here?
   a) ☐ Yes, everyone is really friendly.
   b) ☐ No, I can't make it.
   c) ☐ No, I haven't been here long.

They were alone in the lift and Hunter felt his hunter's instincts rise. He was an agent and had incredibly attractive, lightly greying temples. His landlord, Mr Jones, had recently said, "With such pretty little greying temples you can get anything you want, Hunter. You've got a rascals' charm."
"Pretty" hadn't pleased Hunter. But maybe Mr Jones was right about the rest.
"Seven", said a voice next to him. The woman stepped out of the lift in front of Hunter, to make it easier for his laden to exit down self. "Rascal's charm", he thought and followed her, sure of victory. At the same time he got tangled in the blue and yellow scarf which dangled from the box.
"Whoa, almost a highflier," she laughed and watched him as he righted himself by skilfully manoeuvring the scarf. Then she turned around and stepped back into the lift wiggling her hips.

Übung 10: Unterstreichen Sie das „schwarze Schaf"!

ÜBUNG 10 !

1. pretty, attractive, handsome, ugly, beautiful
2. scarf, gloves, bikini, hat, socks
3. speak, laugh, talk, say, utter
4. move, manoeuvre, push, pull, leave
5. lift, escalator, stairs, pavement
6. landlord, tenant, owner, rent, lease

Agent Sid Newport poked his head round Hunter's door. Like Hunter, he was around 1.85 m tall, only stockier. He had a round face and the casually cut jacket he wore over his T-shirt lent him the informal touch of an experienced secret agent. The usual mischievous expression was missing from his eyes today.

"Have you already met the old monster?" he shouted gutturally. He came closer to Hunter's desk, moved some papers aside and weighed the trophy with the silver ball quickly and appraisingly in his hand.

"I'd rather shoot you with this bullet!"

"Put it down, that's my cricket trophy as champion in the Secret Service tournament." Hunter interrupted brusquely and snatched the trophy from his friend.

"Treasures like that will have been won for a long time, my friend. Who knows how long we've got left here? Until tomorrow? Or perhaps until the weekend?"

! ÜBUNG 11

Übung 11: Setzen Sie die Verben in die richtige Zeitform!

Hunter (1. understand) ________________ what Sid (2. want) __________. Since the Secret Service _________ (3. begin) _________ downsizing and (4. start) _________ its efficiency campaign, hardly any of the older agents (5. be) __________ safe from becoming redundant. Most of those who the academy finished with (6. hand) __________ in their notice in the last few months. All were experienced and aged between 45 and 55: Men and women in their prime. Hunter (7. be) ________ especially sorry about Patricia. She (8. be) __________ his team partner for years.

During that terrible business in Italy she (9. help) ______________

him come back to life. He (10. visit) ______________

her once since her redundancy. She now (11. give)

______________ aerobics and yoga classes for frustrated house-

wives and househusbands. It (12. almost break) ______________

his heart.

Sid was from the "4th Alert Division", a quick response team for external missions.
"I've got some info from HQ about who's put us in this position." With this, Sid brought his friend back to reality.
"Callaghan has given up her active service career. It's left the likes of us speechless."
To emphasise his point, he took the end of Hunter's scarf and whirled it backwards and forwards a few times. Then he started his tale:
"Listen to this: best in her year at the Secret Service Academy, various honours from national and international operations, well-versed in all Asian combat techniques, even in some that the Asians themselves don't know. Rapid rise through the departments in HQ and she's been in the boss's seat for a week now."
Sid's litany had made Hunter furious.
"She's a very pushy person. She should come over. I'll tell her. She's probably slept her way to the top. They all do it. Because of that woman, I'm stuck here on desk duty. Promotion to Head of 'Internal Affairs'. Damn it, what am I doing here? Should I take down the nasty remarks of my colleagues and then give out tickets? Or try to do good and form loving bonds between them?"

Übung 12: Finden Sie die richtige Bedeutung!

ÜBUNG 12

1. mates
   a) ☐ friends
   b) ☐ colleagues

2. to nab
   a) ☐ to prod with the finger
   b) ☐ to catch

3. bumfluff
   a) ☐ hair on your bottom
   b) ☐ light, downy hair on your face

4. the likes of us
   a) ☐ people like us
   b) ☐ things we like

5. well-versed
   a) ☐ knows a lot of poetry
   b) ☐ had a lot of experience and practice in

6. pushy
   a) ☐ encourages others
   b) ☐ too assertive

"Where a person is happy, he can be at peace."
The laughing woman from the lift came into Hunter's office. He took his arm down jerkily and shoved the trophy behind the scarf, which was lying on the table. Pretending concentration, he lowered his gaze and began sorting the papers lying all over his desk. He

stacked them into two piles. He wanted to turn to the visitor smoothly with a confident smile.

"To what do we owe the honour? Or has the hang woman come to exact the death sentence?"

At Sid's remark the smile died on Hunter's face.

A thought flashed through his mind, "That can't be right …"

The woman in the suit remained in the door. She sucked air audibly in through her nose, stood up straight and moved her chest well formed, Hunter noted, forward. She flexed her shoulders. The stiletto heels of her pumps positively ground into the floor. She breathed out. Under the neat tailored suit jacket her chest sank down, only to rise again. She hissed as she quickly filled her lungs with air and said piercingly:

"Newport, if you don't get your ass out of here quick smart, I can guarantee that tomorrow you'll be back in the queue outside the job centre."

She sat down, speaking more quietly, but in an ice cold, measured tone:

"But who wants to take on an agent who's past his sell by date? Especially one your age?"

With those final words, she wrinkled the corners of her mouth. Under thin, plucked stripes of eyebrows her grey eyes had been staring directly at Sid the whole time. Now she slowly looked away as if she was giving him absolution.

"Anyway, have a nice day," Sid muttered from between gritted teeth. He turned and went past her with his head held high and disappeared in the direction of his office. Hunter and Callaghan gazed after him. A door outside slammed hard, but didn't click shut. A male voice uttered a muffled curse and slammed the door shut again.

ÜBUNG 13 !

Übung 13: Formulieren Sie die Sätze höflicher!

1. Newport, get back to your office!

2. Sit down in your seat!

3. Shut that door!

4. Stand up when I'm talking to you!

5. Stop laughing!

6. Eat your dinner!

A friendly smile met Hunter. Without the slightest sign of recognition, the woman in the suit stretched out her hand to the agent. "Now officially, Hunter. My name is Dr Callaghan. You can call me Callaghan."

ÜBUNG 14 !

Übung 14: Um welche Berufe handelt es sich?

1. She stays at home and looks after her children.

2. She is in charge of the workers.

____

3. He investigates national and international crimes.

____

4. He works in an office doing paperwork.

____

It was exactly four in the afternoon when Hunter looked at his digital watch, for what was probably the hundredth time. Time was standing still. Hunter was bored – probably for the first time in his career as an agent. Usually his missions involved coordinating meetings and tracking. And today? This morning he had emptied his locker in his old department's team changing room, the 5th Rapid Response. In the lift, he had flirted for a brief moment with a woman who had turned to be his new – very unpleasant – boss. Otherwise? Nothing. In the meantime the few things from his locker had been distributed round his new office. A few folders and files sat sparsely on high shelves. His photos from the display cupboard in the changing room lay in the lowest drawer of his new desk. He pulled it open and took the pictures out.

Übung 15: Schreiben Sie die Zahlen aus!

ÜBUNG 15 !

1. 5th ____

2. £342.90 ____

3. 7.01.04 ____

4. 1.70 m ______________________________

5. 10,672 ______________________________

6. $0.50 ______________________________

“Welcome!” exclaimed a happy sounding young man at his door. With a quick movement, Hunter threw the photos back into the drawer and shut it with his shin. Then he folded both hands in front of him on the desk. He wasn’t used to sitting behind a desk. The position he was in made him cramped and he took his right hand off the table, turned his upper body to the left, leaned backwards in his chair and crossed his legs. His right hand stayed raised in the air. He couldn’t spontaneously think of anything to do with it.
The young man at the door took it as a greeting. He tapped three times on the doorframe with the knuckle of his forefinger. With each tap, his head nodded in acknowledgement and his eyebrows moved together above his remarkable nose.

Übung 16: Wählen Sie die passende Aussage aus!

1. Hunter just solved a case.
   a) ☐ Well done!
   b) ☐ Welcome!

2. A friend of Hunter’s had a baby.
   a) ☐ Cheers!
   b) ☐ Congratulations!

3. Hunter and Newport are out for a drink.
   a) ☐ Cheers!
   b) ☐ Good day!

4. Friends have just arrived at your party.
   a) ☐ Come in!
   b) ☐ Come on!

He entered the room with one large step. His narrow face still showed an expression of utmost happiness and respect. His brown eyes wandered back and forth between Hunter, the floor in front of the desk and the bare walls.

Übung 17: Setzen Sie die Wörter an der richtigen Stelle ein!
(amused, simultaneously, extremely, retro, colossal, heard, dragged, cord)

Finally they stopped at the green plant pot which he was holding in his hand. With the other hand he supported the 1. __________ clay pot. The plant leant dangerously to one side. The young man was trying 2. ____________________ not to drop the leather file he had jammed under his right arm. A heavy plastic bag 3. ____________________ at his wrist. The handle cut deep into his skin. Hunter decided not to leave his right hand lost in the air any longer and laid it on the knee of his crossed legs. This 4. ____________________ thin and extremely tall character 5. ______________ him. He estimated him to be 1.90 m or more. The beige 6. ______________ trousers which didn't quite reach his shoes had something quite stylish about them.

"Perhaps he's going for 7. ________________ style?" Then a different thouhgt crossed Hunter's mind, "Or is he worried about floods?"

"Percy Horn. My name is Horn. Percy. Junior Agent Trainee. I'm so pleased to meet you Mr Hunter. I've already 8. ______________ so much about you."

Percy spoke extremely correctly. Then he took a step towards Hunter's desk. With both hands, he held out the pot plant. At the same time, he hit the dangling bag against the front of the desk. The plant tipped and Hunter grabbed at it bravely. He seized leaves and stalk. The roots came after them. A tangled bundle stuck out of Hunter's fist as he sank back down in his chair. The files had slipped from Percy's grasp and fallen on to his trainers. His thin face contorted for a moment. When he became aware of Hunter's amused glance he gave a small, embarrassed cough.
"Yes, that's what I'd call a successful start to working together."
He pointed with a long, thin finger at the rest of the plant, which hung limply over Hunter's hand.
"You would have had to harvest it sooner or later. It's basil. I thought I'd bring something practical. You can season sandwiches with basil. On mozzarella and tomato. Or on cheese. And if we eat sandwiches together, then …"

ÜBUNG 18 !

Übung 18: Ordnen Sie richtig zu!

1. Welcome to the department.
2. Did you find it alright?

3. I've brought you something for your office.
4. It's nice to meet you at last.
5. I think we've met before.
6. I hope you'll enjoy your time here.

a) ☐ It's nice to meet you too.
b) ☐ Thank you, it's nice to be here.
c) ☐ It's lovely, thank you.
d) ☐ Have we? Where was that?
e) ☐ Thank you, so do I.
f) ☐ No problem, I had good directions.

Up to this point, Hunter had listened to the performance in silence. "Parcy, or whatever you're called, shut up for a minute. What is all this? What do you want from me?"

First, Percy looked taken aback, then a little offended: "Dr Callaghan chose me for your team. 'Internal Affairs'. I'm supposed to start my traineeship with you."

Hunter's voice became surly: "And who are you to just stroll in and suddenly be on my team? And why don't I know that I have a team at all?"

"No one else is coming. Dr Callaghan thinks two of us are enough for the job."

The momentary defiant expression in the young man's eyes brought a new sense of awkwardness.

"If you don't want … you can definitely sort out something else, I don't have to do it. I'm fresh from the Academy and up to now, I haven't worked in any area. It's all the same to me. And forgive me for the incident with the basil, but I didn't know you didn't like sandwiches."

Übung 19: Unterstreichen Sie die Adjektive!

Here Hunter interrupted him. The lad standing opposite him in his too-short trousers made him sad. The round cut of his patterned Norwegian sweater with red-green diamonds showed much too much of his long neck, rising thinly from his shoulders. Everything about Percy Horn was long and gangling. Hunter suddenly found himself thinking paternal thoughts. He moved from his casual position behind the desk. He wiped his hand with his handkerchief and leant across the table to Percy.
"I'm sorry. I didn't mean it. About the basil and everything."

Übung 20: Finden Sie ein Synonym im Text!

1. rest of ______________________
2. sniff ______________________
3. wait ______________________
4. position ______________________
5. earnest ______________________
6. filthy ______________________
7. nice ______________________
8. lengthily ______________________

Hunter threw the dirty paper tissue on top of the remains of the plant, which he had already put in the waste paper basket under the desk. He noticed how Percy's face and stance slowly relaxed. It gave the experienced agent a pleasant feeling of doing some good

and he sat back down magnanimously. “So today I’m not just head of the ‘Internal Affairs’ department but also a team leader.”
Percy wasn’t sure whether Hunter was really serious about what he was saying. He hesitated a moment, before replying to his superior. The plastic bag slid to the ground, and he absentmindedly massaged the bruise on his wrist. The young man sniffled briefly and Hunter handed him the pack of pocket tissues which were lying on the table. Percy took one out, nodded his thanks and blew long and laboriously with many wipings, foldings and further foldings.
“Where’s your office going to be then?” asked Hunter in a friendly ‘small talk’ tone. Percy sniffled again into what space was left in his handkerchief, crumpled it up and stuffed it into the pocket of his cord trousers. “Dr Callaghan thought I should put my desk in here with you. Then it’ll be easier for the team to communicate.”

Übung 21: Beantworten Sie die Fragen zum Text!

ÜBUNG 21 !

1. Why is Percy in Hunter’s office?

____

2. What does Percy bring Hunter as a welcome present?

____

3. What happens to the present?

____

4. Why did Percy think it would be a good present?

____

The following morning Hunter didn't have the usual spring in his step as he came down the stairs. His old elan was missing.

"Mr Hunter, you look ill," his landlord, Edwin Jones, announced at the door. Jones was there to change a bulb in the stairwell. He moved his ladder to the side to allow access to the door.
"You look like you've been partying hard. Where were you yesterday?" The originally teasing tone of the old man suddenly changed to concern.
"Or has something happened?"

! ÜBUNG 22

Übung 22: Wählen Sie die passende Antwort aus und kreuzen Sie diese jeweils an!

1. Are you alright?
   a) ☐ No, I feel terrible.
   b) ☐ No. it's wrong.

2. What's wrong with you?
   a) ☐ I've got to get to work.
   b) ☐ I had too much to drink last night.

3. Can I do anything to help?
   a) ☐ No, it's OK.
   b) ☐ My head really aches.

Since Hunter had moved into the two-storey brick house on the edge of London, Jones had endeavoured to look out for his welfare. And not just his. The 70-year-old landlord passed the time busily doing caretaker's jobs. Most of the jobs could have easily been done by his tenants. But for Jones, tackling these jobs wasn't just something that came naturally, it was almost a passion. Since his early youth, he had had a nose for criminals. For example, while decalcifying Rosi Carpenter's sink, he had found out why she was divorced from womanising Mr Carpenter. Now she lived with her young daughter Ginny in the attic flat. Underneath lived Miss Windhall, an old spinster in her early sixties. She was a tricky case. Jones was pretty sure that the old woman had maintained links to the Russian Secret Service. Allegedly she had spent a year in Moscow.

The apartment next to Miss Windhall belonged to his special case: Hunter.

Jones had taken up the cause of finding Hunter a woman. It wasn't good to be living alone in your mid-forties. At almost 1.85 m, slim and in good shape, Hunter didn't look too bad.

Übung 23: Finden Sie sinnvolle Synonyme und fügen Sie diese in die Lücken unten ein!

1. His face was filled with (concern) ______________________.

2. He looked very tall and (slim) ______________________ in his tailored suit.

3. Underneath the young couple lived an (old) ________________ spinster.

4. His neighbours were very (loud) ____________________.

5. It was very (tricky) _________________ to mend the old lamp.

6. The woman in the top flat has a (young) ______________ girl.

Hunter greeted him: “Good morning, Mr Jones. Are you worried about us being able to see?”
Jones wiped the lightbulb on the breast pocket of his blue overalls. He was obviously relieved that Hunter was in the mood for jokes.
“So it was a night of wine, women and song then?” he said snidely.
“You have to have some fun sometimes,” grinned Hunter from red, swollen eyes giving an impression of contentment. Tonight he’d quietly and secretly remove yesterday evening’s empty wine bottle from the bins. Hopefully Jones wouldn’t catch him at it and take him to task again.
“Be careful, Redeye.” With that, Jones sent him on his way. And as Hunter opened the door and turned to go: “Don’t spend your money unwisely. As a tax-payer I’ll be insulted.”

Hunter smiled resignedly, waved quickly and went. In the beginning, it had seemed funny to Hunter that the Secret Service had made him take on a false identity working in the finance industry. In the meantime, he found it quite amusing. Other colleagues had far worse. Somebody had disguised Wayne Campbell as a deputy shift leader in a toy factory and Sid Newport as an employee of the London Underground Complaints Office … poor guy.

ÜBUNG 24 !

Übung 24: Wie lauten die Fragen in der richtigen Reihenfolge?

1. out was evening your how?

____

2. enjoy at did party yourself you the?

____

3. think did music you what the of?

---

4. did you when get home?

---

5. there who did see you?

---

6. to have today do work you?

Percy Horn must have already been in the office for hours. Everything looked different.

"A very good morning to you Mr Hunter. Or should I call you boss? Or chief agent?"

The talkativeness of the young man, who was wearing beige cord trousers and trainers again, but had decided on a Norwegian jumper with green and blue diamonds, was too much for Hunter.

"You look tired," continued Percy.

Hunter shrugged his shoulders. It wasn't the first time he'd heard that today.

"Just a second, I'll be right back," said Percy to the man sitting in front of him. With a giant stride he left the room, turned once at the door and smiled cheerfully at Hunter.

"Yes!" he heard, as if Percy was encouraging himself. With a brisk movement he turned off down the corridor between the offices.

*Übung 25: Formulieren Sie die Sätze mit **let's (let us)**!*

1. We should start work.

____

2. Shall we have a cup of tea first?

____

3. Now we'll look at these files.

____

4. We have to look at the documents very carefully.

____

Hunter threw his rucksack down beside the desk. He didn't have a briefcase – he was an agent. He squashed himself into the chair behind him. His leg knocked against the waste paper bin. Another smaller desk stood to the right corner of the desk. The corners of both desks touched. Obviously, Percy already had the place furnished comfortably. Instead of a normal chair, an ergonomic seat like a rubber ball was waiting for him. Two picture frames were arranged on either side of the computer. One was like an oversized pear made of light-blue plastic. The bottom was rounded and when Hunter leaned forwards and touched the desk, the pear on Percy's desk began to wobble back and forth.

Übung 26: Ersetzen Sie die Verkürzungen durch ganze Wörter!

1. He hasn't had a cup of tea yet this morning.

____

2. The office doesn't look very big with two desks in it.

3. We'll have a coffee break soon.

4. Let's work on the reconaissance files.

5. I can't function without a coffee.

6. We're getting somewhere on this case.

"'Morning has broken' or 'The early bird catches the worm'?" asked Percy. He had returned to the office with two coffee mugs. One had 'Morning has broken' written in curly gold script on white background. The other showed a brightly coloured cartoon bird – in pyjamas and holding a toothbrush – roaring past a worm in a convertible. Hunter decided spontaneously on the worm and found his decision was right as he took his first sip.

Übung 27: Wie lautet die richtige Bedeutung des Idioms?

1. The early bird catches the worm.
   a) ☐ If you arrive early you can have what you want.
   b) ☐ If you were a bird you'd eat worms for breakfast.

2. He's got his feet on the ground.
   a) ☐ He is standing and ready to go.
   b) ☐ He is reliable and not a dreamer.

3. He's in the driving seat.
   a) ☐ He is always the driver on missions.
   b) ☐ He is in charge.

4. They're armed to the teeth.
   a) ☐ They have lots of weapons.
   b) ☐ Their teeth are sharp enough to be used as weapons.

Two files were waiting for him on his desk. He quickly put one to the side. It was a report about sexual harassment in the workplace. He had reckoned on receiving this kind of junk when he had been 'promoted' to head of 'Internal Affairs'. Office infighting, intrigue and pettiness. Already the names of the people involved showed it was a petty matter. The second file held Hunter's attention. A complaint of excessive brutality within the Service. Such reports were rare in the Secret Service. There were known rules of conduct – even for eliminating enemies. Cruelty was to be avoided at all costs and showed a weakness in those who used it.

In general, agents held back their emotions when they were on a mission. They would have to kill people. These rules were flexible though, and objectively, you could judge whether the situation required special action. A basically honourable agent didn't use these loopholes but generally respected the rules of conduct.

Recently, Hunter had heard of encroachments on this code. Of cases in which torture had been used and enemies left not only unfit for battle, but also tortured to death. He could only vouch for the '5th Rapid Response Team', of which he had, until last week, been a part. However, some guys from the 4th and 7th didn't trust him. Many agents had shadowy careers as professional killers behind them. God only knew how they'd ended up in the Secret Service.

Übung 28: Welche Gegenteile gehören zusammen?

ÜBUNG 28 !

1. promoted	☐ kind
2. quickly	☐ rigid
3. cruel	☐ passive
4. petty	☐ slowly
5. flexible	☐ important
6. active	☐ demoted

Disgusted, Hunter put down his coffee cup next to the open file. "That's horrible.", he said, more to himself than to Percy who was banging deliberately away at the keyboard of his PC. Percy jumped up. Was the coffee too strong? His superior distracted the young agent by murmuring,
"What's been done here is simply unbelievable."
He stared dumbly at the photos from forensics. He leafed once more through the small package.
Then he picked out one of the pictures and tapped his finger again and again on one point. His fingernail made a notch in the glossy paper of the photograph. Hunter noticed this and stopped. He didn't want to make the damage to the woman's body worse. She hadn't been that young. He could tell from the grey, permed hair that fell to the nape of her neck. However, she wasn't old either. The skin on her naked body was still taut, only her bottom noticeably wide and flabby – out of place on the almost delicate frame. She lay

outstretched on her stomach. The picture showed her from hairline to toes. Her right leg with its slim ankle was slightly bent. Her arm lay close to her body. In her back was a small hole. It came from a bullet. A pool of blood spread out from under her like a bedsheet. The pool didn't reach quite to the top and under her legs the grey linoleum of the floor was clearly recognisable.

He quickly shoved the photograph of the front of the body to the bottom of the pile. He knew what it looked like when a bullet of this type made its exit.

ÜBUNG 29 !

Übung 29: Bringen Sie den Dialog in die richtige Reihenfolge und notieren Sie die Nummerierung!

1. "Did they catch him?"

2. "That's terrible!"

3. "I don't think so."

4. "What happened?"

5. "I know."

6. "Who by?"

7. "She was shot."

8. "Someone broke in."

Lösung: _ _ _ _ _ _ _ _

Übung 30: Setzen Sie die richtige Verbform ein!

He knew the feeling of hope that such a small entry wound (1. can) ______ give. The hope that by simply (2. put) ________ a finger in the smeary point in their flesh you (3. can) ______ save someone. The feeling of relief because the entry wound (4. bleed) ________ so little. And he (5. know) ________ the bleak moment when you (6. turn) _________ over the body. When you (7. look) ________ unprepared straight into the crater the shot (8. rip) ___________ into the stomach, breast or hips on exiting.

He thought of a night in Italy, a heart full of love and a shot bringing blood.
Percy observed him attentively. He had stopped tormenting his PC and now asked, “What have you got there? Some work for us?”
Hunter put the picture on the pile and pushed it across to his assistant with the side of his hand.
“Oh!” came from his side and nothing more.
“Accident at work. She was a witness in our witness protection programme. Anyway she should have been guarded,” explained Hunter. “The report talks about a sudden escalation of the situation. Someone broke into her house. Todd and Marvin were mentioned as guards. They’re both in the 4th, aren’t they?”
Percy’s finger rested above his PC keyboard. A few seconds later Todd and Marvin’s personnel files had appeared simultaneously in two windows on his screen.

"They were in the 4th," he told Hunter. "Now they're assigned to the 3rd 'Elite'. Under Captain Miller. So you won't find much here." He moved his head expectantly from his own monitor to Hunter's. "Miller … the two accused, Todd and Marvin, said that the Captain gave the order to fire and that's all that happened. And he ordered them to go in with a 'Macster 47'."

ÜBUNG 31 !

Übung 31: Setzen Sie das richtige Fragewort ein!

1. ____________________ unit are Todd and Marvin in?
2. ____________________ happened here?
3. ____________________ was in charge?
4. ____________________ was she being hidden?
5. ____________________ did they shoot?
6. ____________________ did she die?

ÜBUNG 32 !

Übung 32: Lesen Sie weiter und unterstreichen Sie die Verben!

Percy let out a whistle. The 'Macster 47' was reserved for the ultimate elite agents and was regarded as a status symbol. How many could say that they had used such a weapon on a mission? Once they met it, the victim didn't stand a chance. On entering the body, the mechanism released a spraying explosive. The bullet set off a minibomb which exploded again. When the bullets went through the body and came out the other side, they left a bloody, fleshy crater behind.

Übung 33: Setzen Sie die Wörter an den richtigen Stellen ein!
(responsible, standard, depot, termination, devastating, operation, respective, equipped)

Anyone using the weapon had to be aware of the 1. ______________ effects. The Secret Service had pondered long over the statutes of their organisation before being forced to develop the weapons as 2. ______________ due to the increasing threat of terrorism, both nationally and internationally. Only 'elite units' would be 3. ______________ with the 'Macster 47'. This mean it was expected they would be 4. ______________ with it. Apart from that, there were instructions when on duty. The 'Macster 47' was only to be taken out of the weapons 5. ______________ on orders from the Captain of the 6. ______________ 'elite unit'. And only on his orders would they be given out in an 7. ______________. Furthermore, an order was required to fire a 'Macster 47'. 'Freedom to shoot' ended with the success of the mission or the 8. ______________ of the operation.

Percy continued: "Then Captain Miller gave the order to fire and his people shot the witness. Probably by mistake. So, one of the two is guilty and we have to find them out."

"Slow down," Hunter warned him. "Why was this weapon given out for a witness protection programme, surely one of thousands that we have in England alone? Why did Miller give order to shoot at everything and anything? What was a Captain doing at simple witness protection scheme?"

Hunter opened some files on his computer. He was digging through the same files that Percy had got information from.
"Otherwise, there's not much." He could only agree with his young colleague. The facts about Miller's family background, career and his units gave little information. His favourite food was noted and his preferred music. All information you would certainly need if you wanted to capture his heart. But what Hunter was looking for were inconsistencies. For him, this CV was too smooth. Everything was just right. Every job in the right order. One change of department. That was nothing unusual, most people changed frequently. Like himself, just last week – to this desk.

"He moved quickly up the career ladder," confirmed Percy who now had Miller's file open on his PC.
"Shall we have another coffee first and then puzzle over things together?" he suggested.
At the word 'coffee' Hunter cheered up. "Percy, you know what, three years ago all our existing data was completely digitised. What do you think of verifying how completely it's been done? I don't really know if you're up to such a difficult job …"
Percy immediately shook his head violently in order to allay Hunter's doubts. Then it occurred to him that he might have confirmed earlier that he wasn't up to the job. Confused, he hesitated a fraction of a second. Then he nodded:
"I'd like to do it anyway. Thank you for putting your trust in me."

Übung 34: Ordnen Sie die Buchstaben zu einem sinnvollen Wort!

1. We caught the (tpulcri) ______________ with DNA evidence.

2. The case isn't solved yet, it's still a bit of a (ysytmre) ________.

3. He was acting very (spcuilsuyois), so they arrested him.

4. The agent was working (vuderreocn) ______________ in a bank.

5. Hunter and Horn were (lonapliteshc) ______________________ detectives.

6. The evidence pointed to one (lisccnouon) __________________.

It took him some time to find the entrance to the archive cellar. As the folders and files were no longer needed, they were stored in catacombs and vaults that stretched for kilometres below the Secret Service building.
Percy went down the stairs quickly. Here in the doorway his momentum deserted him. Not all the lights on the ceiling were working. The light in the corridor was pale. He breathed in the stuffy air from the cellar. His steps echoed eerily off the walls. He looked around for the right door. A squeak startled him. His foot stepped on something soft. Whatever it was scurried past his other leg and disappeared into a hole in the wall.
"Ugh!" he kicked out. Apparently no one had had been down here for quite some time. The young agent pulled himself together. He concentrated on the signs by the doors. Finally he found what he was looking for: Archive Room 456. His hand closed around the metal doorknob.
Crying out he moved it back. His fingers burnt like fire. A shock went through his body. He trembled. What was this? A nasty blister

bulged on the palm of his hand. The young man pressed the blister with the forefinger of his other hand. It burst. Percy whimpered and watched irritatedly as liquid ran over his hand. When he wiped off his hand on his trousers, he ripped off a piece of skin. He cried out. Then he looked more carefully at the lock. A small black box was fastened under the doorknob. Percy discovered a virtually invisible wire snaking round the metal. Carefully, he touched the wire. This time he didn't get a shock. He tugged the wire out of the box and was able to break the connection.

Übung 35: Ordnen Sie den Sätzen die passenden Geräusche zu!

1. A mouse runs across the corridor.	a) ☐ Crack!
2. The door opens slowly.	b) ☐ Bang!
3. Percy drops his torch.	c) ☐ Creak!
4. Someone fires a gun.	d) ☐ Squeak!
5. A door is broken in.	e) ☐ Splat!
6. A mouse falls to the floor.	f) ☐ Crash!

The door to the archive opened inwards. Percy stepped on something soft again. This time it wasn't a mouse. The animal bit his shoe and tugged on it. With a kick he flung it away. It splattered against something hard. The agent breathed deeply. His hand groped for the light switch. Glaring light illuminated the room. Archive Room K456: 'Personnel Files', stretched in front of him like an almost endless corridor. The rat he had just stepped on was stuck to the first filing cabinet. Its jaws were open wide. The hide on its neck was coloured blood red. Its thin, bare tail lay outstretched on the floor. It wasn't moving any more.

Percy advanced along the corridor. Many other narrower corridors branched off between the metal filing cabinets. Grey cardboard boxes were stacked in storage space. Some had numbers or letters written on them. The majority gave no clue as to their contents. The regular crackling of neon lights above his head gave Percy the comforting certainty that he wasn't quite abandoned.
He took off his Norwegian jumper, folded it carefully and laid it down beside him on the floor. He stuffed the loose bottom of his T-shirt back into the waistband of his trousers. Then he sat down cross-legged on his jumper and pulled the bottom box towards him. Dust tickled his nose. He sneezed and the cellar walls echoed back the sound.

Übung 36: Formulieren Sie die Sätze im Passiv!

1. Percy kicked the rat.

____

2. Bright neon lights lit the cellar.

____

3. The secretary had written numbers on the boxes.

____

4. Dust covered the old cabinets.

____

5. Percy picked up the first file excitedly.

____

Hunter didn't let his consternation show. It was unbelievable what the architect had done with the office. There was nothing, absolutely nothing to remember McCarthy, his previous boss who had retired two months ago, by.
"Oh good, you're here," began Callaghan. She hadn't even asked him to sit down. She was enthroned on a black leather chair. Her upright posture represented complete superiority.
"Sit down Hunter," Callaghan waited until he had lowered himself into one of the two leather chairs opposite. Her manner fit well with her chair, only the chair was smaller and too soft thought Hunter. He sank down and involuntarily slipped back on the backrest. His knees were high in front, his backside hung far too low in the seat cushion. He began to awkwardly to burrow himself out. Callaghan's impatient look accompanied his efforts and he decided to give up trying to extricate himself.

ÜBUNG 37 !

Übung 37: Machen Sie aus dem Adjektiv ein Adverb!

1. unbelievable ____________________
2. previous ____________________
3. good ____________________
4. stylish ____________________
5. hard ____________________
6. high ____________________
7. impatient ____________________
8. careful ____________________
9. fast ____________________

"What do you want from me?" said the agent quietly to himself. "Hunter, as soon as you have the chance bring me the files with the complaint against Miller's boys. We'll leave it be."
Apparently, she was now waiting for him to stand up and leave. Anyway, it didn't seem like Callaghan wanted to talk about anything else.
"Do I understand right?" the agent asked himself. "We've got a witness shot. An important witness I assume. Otherwise she wouldn't have been in the witness protection programme. One of our men kills the woman, by mistake or otherwise, in any case, with our most enormous and most carefully guarded weapon."
At this point, Callaghan intervened, clearly bored by Hunter's musings. She reached absent-mindedly for a stray strand of hair, but missed it. Her chestnut brown haircut sat perfectly. 'Perfectionist streak' concluded Hunter harshly.
"First the poor soul wasn't so important, second she had quite a few skeletons in the closet and third, let me worry about it. You'd be better worrying about your young friend."
She laid both hands on the table. The shoulder pads of her suit bulged upwards and made her look like a rugby player. She seemed to want to stand up, but she stayed where she was.

Übung 38: Unterstreichen Sie das „schwarze Schaf"!

1. interrupt, intervene, stop, request
2. thank, praise, complain, congratulate
3. trivial, worthy, significant, important
4. worried, concerned, disinterested, preoccupied
5. confused, aware, comprehending, clued-up
6. talk, discuss, converse, ignore

Hunter made no move to leave. Instead of leaving the room he said: "I wanted to talk to you about that as well. What should I do with my team, my partner and everything?"
Callaghan sank back in her chair with a feigned maternal sigh.
"Hunter, I think I've adopted the wrong tone here. Make sure that the nitwit comes back out of the cellar. Bring me the files and don't stick your nose into cases which are long filed away and have lapsed."
Hunter was annoyed. He uncrossed his knees with both arms and moved himself forward in the seat. In this position, like a flick knife just before it snapped shut, he bore down on her, saying innocently:
"What has lapsed? Who says that Percy's in the archives?"
"Stop having me on," said Callaghan angrily. Hunter thought this was a bit arbitrary.
"You can be glad you still have a job," she started in again. By pressing the palms of both hands onto his knees, he had finally succeeded in freeing his backside from the chair. He was now sitting on the edge of the seat.
"Enjoy yourself. In two months it's my birthday. Then I'll be that little bit older, and you can rationalise me away more easily."
Now Callaghan also leaned forward. Her hands stayed on the edge of the table, but her face was almost touching Hunter's. He looked into her cold eyes under the plucked brows. The sides of her nose trembled slightly and her cheeks showed tiny dimples when she moved the corners of her mouth upwards. Her perfume streamed towards Hunter, uncomfortably sweet. He felt a sneeze coming on but suppressed it.
"My dear friend!" Callaghan was so close to him he could smell her minty breath through the sickly sweetness of her perfume. "If I want to fire you, I will fire you. It makes no difference how old or

young you feel. You have my leniency and recommendation to thank that you're still here. You know you're near the top of the redundancy list."

Übung 39: Ordnen Sie den Wörtern links ihre passenden Synonyme rechts zu!

1. perfume	☐ pretend
2. tremble	☐ sack
3. adopted	☐ scent
4. nitwit	☐ shake
5. fire	☐ took
6. feign	☐ idiot

Hunter held her gaze. He almost liked this discussion. He smiled and waited for the next attack.

"You weren't ordered into internal duties because you've reached middle age. Your psychological evaluation defies description. In your career as an agent, you've botched up more than an entire unit put together."

Hunter was flattered. He had enrolled in the Academy and decided on this job not least because of the dangerous adventures. Callaghan still had a card up her sleeve.

Übung 40: Welche Bedeutung hat das Idiom?

1. A card up her sleeve
   a) ☐ Very stiff sleeves
   b) ☐ A secret advantage

2. Castles in the air

a) ☐ A good imagination

b) ☐ Unrealistic daydreams

3. To have someone on

a) ☐ To invite someone to your office

b) ☐ To joke or lie

"You have to finally see it. Ever since the events in Italy, you've been finished. Since you've been pining over your little friend, it's been over for you. You're all delusions, castles in the air. And it was all for nothing. The gunrunner's hideout was somewhere completely different. But who could have foreseen that the spaghetti bunny would want to rush to help her lover and put herself in the middle of a shooting range. Shit happens, Hunter."
Hunter rose. He had no reply to this. Without another word, he went to the door. Callaghan's piercing instruction met him once more from behind.
"Bring the files. And get Horn out of the cellar."
Shoulders slumped, Hunter left the room.

ÜBUNG 41 !

Übung 41: Setzen Sie die richtige Präposition in die Lücke ein!

"You'll find it yet Horn," Percy encouraged himself. He was still crouched in the archive cellar looking 1. ________ information on Miller. "Just keep looking. Stay with it. Rome wasn't built 2. ________ a day. Or was it Carthage?" While his mind issued a rallying call, his long, slim finger combed 3. _______ the pages and between the tops of the files.

Percy avoided looking 4. ________ the time. He didn't want to know how long he'd already been down here. His eyes smarted 5. __________ the flickering neon light and a constant sinister rumbling. It was probably the air conditioning.

A clump of dust dislodged itself from a shelf just 6. _______ his head as he pulled down box number 7689. Finally he had reached 'MI – MO'. The file marked 7. _______ Miller's name and identity number was near the beginning. Percy took it out and dug deeper in the box. The name Miller filled an entire file, then was followed 8. _______ Mitchell and Montana.

He heard a sound, as if the cellar door had opened. Startled he put the lid back on the box in front of him. Reacting so quickly he had left Miller's file lying out. He stuffed the whole file into his jumper and sat up.

"Update from Callaghan. Shift your ass upstairs and stop sniffing around here."

Two brawny guys in dark made-to-measure suits with shiny polished shoes appeared in front of him. Under the sleeves of the expensive material bulged impressive muscles. Percy gripped his thinned, crossed legs at the ankle with both hands. Slowly he moved his upper body back and forth.

"Are you sitting on your ears man?" asked one of the troublemakers.

Percy knew him slightly from the Academy, he was two years above. Tremendously loud mouthed and pretty successful in everything to do with hand-to-hand combat, pursuit techniques and target practice. Judging by his appearance, he was a member of an 'elite unit'. They were in the habit of talking gruffly amongst themselves. Percy found himself frankly considering whether he was also keen to become one of the 'elite' and if he was a person who craved adventure. The others were indifferent to him. Both now went behind Percy. Barner or Turner pushed a thick finger into Percy's hair and stroked his head.

Übung 42: Welcher Satz enthält die richtige Zeitform?

1. a) ☐ Percy put the file in his jumper when the men entered the room.
   b) ☐ Percy puts the file in his jumper when the men entered the room.

2. a) ☐ The two men are having huge muscles.
   b) ☐ The two men have huge muscles.

3. a) ☐ He had been in the elite unit for five months.
   b) ☐ He is in the elite unit for five months.

4. a) ☐ Captain Miller considers him one of the elite.
   b) ☐ Captain Miller is considering him one of the elite.

"Do you like that little boy?" he asked. The other one laughed throatily. He stuck a finger in Percy's ear and snorted, "OK, little one?"

Percy took a deep breath and began to turn.

"Guys, this is all great fun. Nevertheless, could we leave it? I'm meditating."

The idea seemed almost inspired to him. Meditating in the cellar; no one could have anything against that. The stroking of his head actually began to stop. The finger was taken out of his ear. Percy relaxed.

An icy hand chopped down hard on his shoulder. Before he could even put pressure on the pain, the guy he didn't know whacked him in the face. Percy's cheeks burned.

One of the two twisted his arm up behind his back and pulled him to his feet. A strained gasp escaped from Percy's lips.

"Show me your tummy," purred the guy behind him and tugged on the arm twisted behind his back.

Percy's body bent hollow. The other guy took advantage and hit him in the stomach. Percy felt the hard, flat shoe sole below his stomach. He choked. He received a blow to the back which forced his body quickly forwards. Arms gripped under his shoulders, hands pulled on his T-shirt and finally the muscle men heaved him to the floor.

Übung 43: Welche Körperteile benötigen Sie für die verschiedenen Kampfarten?

1. kick ____________________
2. chop ____________________
3. knee ____________________
4. punch ____________________

ÜBUNG 43 !

5. poke ______________________

6. elbow ______________________

7. headbutt ______________________

8. hit ______________________

Percy kicked out with his feet. He wanted to throw in one of the karate kicks that he'd learnt in the Academy. He hit the shin of one of the attackers. But he didn't seem very impressed. He pulled his victim's arm higher. Percy's shoulder socket creaked threateningly. The second guy gave the young agent a kick in the behind. The sole of his shoe crashed against Percy's coccyx. A sharp pain rent Percy's body right from bottom to top. He felt terrible. He had surrendered over nothing. His knees gave way. His torturer hit him from behind. Percy fell face first hard on to the stone floor.
"Now you see who's won!" jeered his one time colleague from the Academy.
"We don't like to see this rummaging around, darling," said the other one.
"Especially not by guys like you who only wriggled their way in here through nepotism. Thank you so much Uncle Vernon or do you have to thank the parliamentary speaker?"
His colleague reprimanded him, "Josh, that doesn't belong here. Let's move."
"Oh, but it does belong here. Because of this arsehole I had to wait a year for a place in the Academy. Do you know what a year means for an agent?" returned the other.
The answer came quickly and clearly.
"You poor thing. Have you cashed in on it enough … that you waited a year for your place at the Academy?"

Percy followed the conversation as if through a haze. So, Uncle Vernon. He would worry about that later. Every bone in his body hurt. He painfully scrapped himself up only to sink down again quickly as a sharp pain spread out from his stomach. He doubled up, looking reproachfully at his torturers. The two were fighting more seriously and Barner or Turner poked at the muscle-bound chest of the other with his forefinger to strengthen his argument. As their victim began to wheeze his way upright, they left each other alone.

"Get lost, wimp," hissed one of them. Percy bundled up his jumper and limped hurriedly out the door.

Übung 44: Was sagen Sie in den folgenden Situationen?

1. Someone keeps hitting you.
   a) ☐ "Leave me alone!"
   b) ☐ "Leave me lonely!"

2. You are in a four against one situation.
   a) ☐ "I wave a white flag!"
   b) ☐ "I surrender!"

3. You hit your attacker.
   a) ☐ "Feel that!"
   b) ☐ "Take that!"

"Are you busy Hunter?"

The question made the agent jump. He sat behind his desk, head bent deep under the edge of the tabletop. Up until then, he had been hectically rummaging in the lowest drawer where he kept things safe from his previous locker. 'Kept safe' was the right expression. During the move, he had thrown the pictures in with out paying attention. Now he'd never find them in this mess. It had to be there – the photo of Gina with the dark curls and black eyes. His Gina, or almost his Gina. Gina from Naples.

The visitor remained patiently in the door until Hunter finally dragged himself out from under the table.

"You startled me," the agent greeted the woman in a pale twinset and blue stonewashed jeans.

Norma Sanders called happily, "What happened to always ready?" and walked uninvited into the room. She dragged Percy's ergonomic chair, or rubber ball, out from behind the desk. As she rolled the chair in front of Hunter's desk she remarked,

"A bit cosy for you? Eh, boys?"

Boyishly she swung a leg over the ball and placed herself on it. She hopped a few times, like a child on a spacehopper, until she settled herself in a comfortable position.

ÜBUNG 45 !

Übung 45: Bilden Sie Gegenteile durch das Anfügen eines Präfixes!

1. patient ____________________
2. important ____________________
3. legal ____________________
4. attention ____________________
5. regular ____________________
6. happy ____________________

7. comfortable ______________________

8. violent ______________________

Hunter observed Norma. Grey hair stood up in a wild fashion from her head. Hunter guessed she was in her mid-fifties. But many colleagues maintained she was older.
“I can save you loads of work. What do I get for it?” The small person on the rubber ball waited for Hunter’s response. She grinned, smoothing out the wrinkles in her face and only a well-defined dimple still showed on her cheeks.
“OK, I see. You’re a bit stubborn today,” she diagnosed.
Hunter realised that he hadn’t said anything for quite some time.
“Please, Norma. If you could help me with some speech therapy …” They both laughed.

Übung 46: Ersetzen Sie die Wörter durch ihre Synonyme!

ÜBUNG 46 !

With an air of importance, Norma (1. presented with) ______________ Hunter a blue spring folder that she had had in her hand the whole time. He took the folder and started (2. to leaf) ______________ through it, while Norma sat down and began to explain.

“Yesterday morning, Todd came to me and told me about the complaint. He said he couldn’t keep quiet any longer. He had (3. to talk to) ______________ someone. I told him I am not only a

Secret Service psychologist, but that I am also the soul of discretion. (4. To start with) _______________, he was a bit wary. These kind of confessions come from the pressure that dominates many of the units here. It's no coincidence. So there poor Todd sat in front of me, giving me his version of events."

Hunter nodded in acknowledgement and (5. glanced at) _______________ Todd's statement. He looked at Norma.

"You can read about the details later," she went on. "But I have been told that Miller, Todd and Marvin (6. have prospects) _______________ of getting a special briefing soon. That's why they had to get used to using the 'Macster 47'.

The pair wanted to do the nightshift on the farm and do some shooting practice in the barn. All without Captain Miller's knowledge. It must have made them pretty nervous.

At the same time, they killed not only the two people who broke in, but also the witness who they were protecting, Mary Weston. Todd had met her."

Norma bent forward from the chair and cleared a space in the paper that lay in front of Hunter.

"The break-in was something to do with Lynton and Vandermer. Remember the case? With her testimony, Mary Weston put two weapons dealers away for life. This week they were both released."

Triumphantly she put her finger on the page and looked at Hunter eagerly.

"Was she really such an important witness that the Secret Service

had to protect her? Aren't less important people a job for the police usually?"
"No. Lynton and Vandermer were big fish in international weapons trading." The psychologist cleared away the papers. "Don't ask me. The bosses here will already know what to do."
She lifted herself from the chair and leaned against the wall. The ball bounced away and rolled back to her.
"Now enjoy yourself Hunter. This thing is finished for you. Todd has owned up." She put a hand to her forehead in a military salute. "Stay obedient, that's it."

Hunter thanked her and shook her hand. "You're one in a million," he praised.
"If you need anything, you know where to find me. I also mean you personally," she replied.
The agent answered hastily.
"You're catching the same thing as Callaghan. My psyche is perfectly in order."
"If you say so. And don't let the old bitch upset you."
Norma waved briefly and disappeared thorough the door.

Übung 47: Wie lauten die Antworten zu den Fragen? Ordnen Sie die Ziffern den richtigen Buchstaben zu!

1. Would you mind repeating that?
2. Is that clear?
3. Have you got it?
4. Sorry, you've lost me.
5. Are you still with me?
6. Sorry, I didn't catch the last part.

a) ☐ Clear as mud!

b) ☐ Where did you get confused?

c) ☐ Yes, I think I understand …

d) ☐ OK, I'll repeat it.

e) ☐ No problem.

f) ☐ Yes, I'm still following you.

Hunter looked after her for a long moment. Then he buried himself in the folder in front of him. For him, the past wasn't finished like it was for the psychologist. Many inconsistencies still existed. Why had Callaghan wanted to remove him from the case? Why had Miller allowed his people to use such sensitive weapons? Why didn't the agents nab two weapon dealers, but kill a witness instead?
Percy groaned as Hunter applied the cold compress. The experienced agent had placed him in his chair. Ergonomic balls weren't useful in these types of emergencies. The young man held his stomach with his slim hands. It took a while until Hunter could get out of him about what had happened. His anger grew as Percy told his story. He was ready to rush off immediately and give these brutal colleagues what for. Or even better – as Head of the 'Internal Affairs' Department – to string them up. But for that he'd need clearance from his boss, so he could forget it.

People from Miller's 'elite unit'. "This name is popping up constantly," grumbled Hunter. "Miller, Miller, Miller. What is it about this guy?"

Percy groaned again. Still in pain he was reaching awkwardly for his jumper which lay on the edge of the tabletop. He unrolled it and presented his superior with his loot.

"From the archive. Miller's file," he said.

For a moment, the other man was perplexed. Then his expression slowly brightened. Hunter smiled astonishedly and finally said, "Percy, you're a shrewd one!", now looking really happy.

Übung 48: Wie lautet die richtige Bedeutung der Idiome?

ÜBUNG 48 !

1. You're a shrewd one!
   a) ☐ You are good at hiding things.
   b) ☐ You are cleverer than I expected.

2. You're a fount of knowledge!
   a) ☐ You know lots of useful information.
   b) ☐ You are always talking about how much you know.

3. You're the cat's whiskers!
   a) ☐ You're just perfect.
   b) ☐ You're an expert on animals.

4. You're like a bad penny!
   a) ☐ You are always spending money.
   b) ☐ You keep reappearing all over the place.

Contrary to his expectations, the man opposite didn't react happily to this praise.

"It's OK, you can save it. I know why I'm here. 'Vitamin B', the uncle in the Ministry gives his nephew a little present and fulfills his lifelong dream. And the stupid nephew thinks he's done it all himself. Damn it."

Hunter smiled even wider down at Percy.

"Where did you hear that?"

"From the brute who messed me about. And it sounds pretty close to the truth," explained the young man.
Hunter stepped closer behind his colleague. Percy's thin shoulders trembled slightly.
"Now you're not a sissy," began Hunter. "It makes no difference how you get into the Secret Service. You're in. And you stay there too. Be happy that you've got 'Vitamin B'. Other people don't. That's just the way it is! Let's forget about this rubbish and talk in plain English."
Percy threw a doubtful look behind him at the energetic looking man.
"And you know what? Let's not put up with any more. Not from any Callaghans or Millers and whatever the others are called. We'll defend ourselves. Give me the file. I want to have a proper look at it."
Resolutely, he took the papers from Percy, reaffirming his praise for his colleague by punching him on the damaged shoulder, at which Percy groaned in pain and left the office.

! ÜBUNG 49

Übung 49: Wie lauten die Sätze in der richtigen Reihenfolge?

1. doubtful his frequently about ability Percy as is agent an.

____

2. often Hunter confuse Percy things does that.

____

3. bored office Hunter sits day gets and every his in.

____

4. case they today information found new the some on.

5. Percy cellar attacked went after into he soon was the.

6. drinks morning hardly Hunter the coffee in ever.

Übung 50: Unterstreichen und korrigieren Sie die nicht dazugehörenden Sätze!

ÜBUNG 50 !

Hunter's spaghetti came steaming from the microwave. He burns his tongue biting into the first piece of macaroni. Angrily he has examined the clump of pasta with resounding name of 'Macaroni Sorpresa di Milano' and has pushed his plate away. He took a large gulp of orange juice. The wine he had specially to drink with his pasta would stay in the fridge today. He wanted to stay sober and clear-headed when he went through Miller's file. He was still groping in the dark.
There were simply too many oddities. Apart from that, after a few days in the office, he had been already feeling the urge to do something active. The energy which he usually got rid of in daily training or on external missions being to be used to shed some light on the case. He opened the file and began to read.
It was long past midnight when he finished reading. Along with the operations Miller had personally been involved in, the file also included information about which orders he had given and when. This guy had signed a lot of reports and orders in his career. Hunter

sighed and laid another report on the pile of material he had already looked through. It dealt with a case Hunter only vaguely remembered. He had almost forgotten it.

Years ago, the family of an agent had been killed in a fire. At the time of the fire, the father had been on a mission for the Secret Service. The investigation had placed him and other unknown persons under suspicion of murder. The autopsies of the mother and child showed no evidence of violence. At the time, Captain Montgomery had added his signature below Miller's report. Hunter glanced fleetingly at the photos of the corpses. He spared himself from looking at things like that. He breathed in sharply.
The mother's burnt leg could be somewhat identified. It was broken at the same angle as the body in yesterday's picture. The witness that Todd had shot.

ÜBUNG 51 !

Übung 51: Wie lauten die Substantive zu den Verben?

1. to investigate

____

2. to suspect

____

3. to murder

____

4. to perpetrate

____

5. to witness

6. to police

Edwin Jones called to his dog. He held the dog's lead in his hand and was dressed for an autumn morning stroll. The dog simply didn't want to move.
Suddenly, the dog jumped up, wagged its tail and stormed past its owner in the direction of the stairwell. Jones turned in resignation and shrugged his shoulders. Sudden mood changes were normal for Sammy. Ginny and her mother were coming down the stairs. Sammy waited, wagging his tail and rubbed up against Ginny's legs when the little girl petted him. He loved to be stroked behind the cars by her small fingers.
Rosie said hello to the landlord. Hunter came out of his flat door. Ginny's mother went back up a few steps towards him. She didn't want Mr Jones to understand every word that passed between them.
"Good morning," she said. "How would you like to have dinner with me? But only if you've got time. You're clearly very busy …"
Hunter put on his most charming smile and said:
"How can I refuse? I'd love to! When's good for you?"
"Seven o'clock?" asked Rosie. "It's Ginny's bath night. She always floods the entire bathroom." Rosie smiled as she said this and glanced quickly down at the half-landing where her daughter was devotedly petting Sammy.
"I'll start as soon as I've got Ginny out of the bath. I'm making roast lamb with mint sauce."
Hunter showed his anticipation by running his tongue over his lips.

"Till tonight then." He left her and went past Ginny and Jones with a wave.

Hunter stepped through the main door into to a foggy London autumn morning.

Übung 52: Bringen Sie die Sätze in die richtige Reihenfolge!

1. visit   me   why   don't   at the weekend   you

____ ?

2. over   for   what   about   lunch   coming

____ ?

3. come   to my birthday party   would   you   to   like

____ ?

4. the art gallery   with   how   about   me   going to   on Thursday

____ ?

5. visiting   what   you   do   the beach   think of

____ ?

6. new exhibition   want   you   do   the   see   to

____ ?

Percy still looked somewhat worse for wear. He was limping slightly and one shoulder hung slightly lower than the other. But even his injuries didn't prevent him from preparing coffee for his boss again today.

"Listen Percy. This is really nice of you, but I'm really a tea drinker," replied Hunter. The young man nodded attentively and went back out of the office with the two mugs.
Hunter felt guilty again. Why couldn't he simply gratefully accept it when someone's intentions were good?
When Percy stepped back into their office on his long, thin legs, all feelings of guilt left Hunter. A grinning Percy with mugs with the colourful tags of the teabags hanging out was too much. Before the young man could launch into an enthusiastic explanation of the pictures on the mugs, Hunter interrupted him.
"Horn, let's leave the morning coffee for today and devote ourselves to the important things in life."
Nevertheless, the young agent sat down on his ball and positioned both mugs demonstratively beside his computer monitor. He ignored his boss and hacked at the keyboard.

Übung 53: Unterstreichen Sie das passende Wort!
Vorsicht! Die Wörter klingen gleich!

1. I can't sea/see the point in investigating this case.
2. I must write/right an email to the officer in charge.
3. I get to the office at eight/ate every morning.
4. I opened the window and a cold wind blue/blew through the office.
5. I knew/new it wasn't as simple as it looked!
6. After being beaten up, I felt very week/weak.
7. Once this case is over, I'd like some piece/peace and quiet.
8. We're going to break/brake this case soon, I can feel it.

"You'd like a bit of new information to chew on?" he asked. Percy just didn't get it. 'Internal Affairs' was, as the name said, a department which dealt with internal events in the Secret Service – also meaning inside the building.

Hunter had already jumped up and grabbed his leather jacket, which he'd laid over the back of his chair. He swung his blue rucksack onto his shoulder and came round the corner of his desk. He took his keychain out of his jacket pocket and threw it to Percy.

"You're going out!"

Confused, Percy picked up the black leather file. He stood up hesitantly. Hunter was already out the door. Percy hurried to follow him, seizing his files from under the table and reaching for one of the teacups with his free hand. He only managed a quick slurp before putting the tea hurriedly back down. The tea went down his windpipe, and he ran outside choking after his boss.

Übung 54: Setzen Sie die richtigen Präpositionen in die jeweiligen Lücken ein!

Hunter waited impatiently 1. _______ Percy in the Secret Service underground garage. He took his rucksack off his shoulder and put it 2. ______ the ground. The zip caught a little but Hunter energetically tore it free. He hadn't felt so much enthusiasm in a long time. He retrieved a half-full bottle of mineral water out of his rucksack and unscrewed the lid. Percy was hurrying 3. ________ his direction, files swinging. Hunter took a large swig, put the bottle

4. ________ and wiped the neck with his hand. The bubbles tickled his nose. The tingling in his nose ran over his whole body. He was looking 5. ____________________ to this mission. Finally back out 6. ________ the office again.

Percy reached the grey estate car panting.
"Sorry, I had to wait for the lift," panted the straggler, "and it had already gone."
He rummaged in the leather folder looking for the right key for the driver's door. Hunter waited impatiently for the beep that showed the doors were open and then sat down in the passenger seat. Strapping himself in, he glanced at his colleague who sat waiting at the steering wheel. Percy sensed Hunter's excitement and allowed himself to be caught up in it. His first real mission. Because Hunter didn't bother to give him instructions about where they were going or which route to follow, Percy decided to go for the most obvious. He turned the key and let the motor start. Very carefully he reversed the car out. Under no circumstances did he want to thoughtlessly damage Hunter's car.
The barrier led out into the centre of London. Percy drove forward, joined the queue of cars and waited for the green light.
"Excuse me for being nosy, but where are we actually going?"
Hunter ignored the quiet, reproachful voice inside telling him that he had remained silent so far about the goal and reason for the journey. He crossed both arms behind his head and made himself as comfortable as possible in the seat. Then he explained:
"We're going to Pontypool. There we're going to visit a police station and a guy I know. Sullivan, Mike Sullivan, formerly of the Secret Service. 'Elite'. Stationed in London. Now in Pontypool."

The traffic moved slowly through the blocked streets. On the left, they passed the British Museum and the University of London and threaded their way through the heavy traffic onto Oxford Street. The streets of Soho were pretty full of traffic this morning. The traffic jams began to clear as they went further south and at Vauxhall Bridge, the traffic flowed quickly in the direction of the suburbs.

ÜBUNG 55 !

Übung 55: Beim Autofahren: Beantworten Sie die Fragen!

1. What has red, yellow and green lights?

____

2. What must you wear in case of accidents?

____

3. What makes the car stop?

____

4. Pontypool is to the South, Scotland is to the …?

____

5. What do you use to plan your route?

____

6. To avoid a fine you must obey the speed …?

____

Hunter reached into the back section of his rucksack, dug around for a few seconds and unearthed a mobile phone. He held it with both hands to his ear as he answered.

"Yes, that's right. Stupid flu. It came on yesterday. Will you manage a whole day without me?" Percy heard his boss say into the speaker. After a short pause, Hunter said, "It wasn't especially great yesterday. Presumably he infected me or I infected him. I don't really know." After another short pause he followed it up with,
"Thanks. Talk to you tomorrow."
Hunter stuffed the mobile back in his rucksack. Looking at the traffic, Percy asked,
"Who was that?"
The man beside him crossed his arms behind his neck, "It was the lovely Callaghan. She was worried about us both."
"You mean…" began the young man, head turning back and forth between Hunter and the street.
"Yes, she doesn't know anything about our little trip. It's better that way. Officially we've both got the flu and you gave it to me."

Übung 56: Beim Telefonieren: Welche Antwort passt?

1. Hello, is Hunter there?
   a) ☐ Speaking!
   b) ☐ Here is Hunter.

2. He's not here, can you …
   a) ☐ answer back?
   b) ☐ call back?

3. Can I speak to Percy?
   a) ☐ Hold on a minute.
   b) ☐ Ring on a minute.

4. Do you know when he'll be back?
   a) ☐ He'll call you later.
   b) ☐ He'll be in at three.

5. I'll try calling later.
   a) ☐ OK, I'll tell him you called.
   b) ☐ OK, I'll tell him to call you.

6. Goodbye.
   a) ☐ We speak us soon.
   b) ☐ Speak to you soon.

Two hours later, they arrived in the small town. They parked the estate car right in front of the police station. Hunter felt good to finally be back in the game. He flexed his knees a few times, gazed at his trainers and grabbed his rucksack strap.

The glass panelled door squeaked quietly when it opened. Hunter held it open until Percy had gone through ahead of him. Then he let it shut with a crash. The glass wobbled. Confused, Hunter looked around him. There was no one in sight.

A shrill, penetrating sound made him jump. Percy shrugged his shoulders apologetically and took his finger off the old-fashioned metal bell under which a sign with 'Please ring' was fastened.

The bell was the only thing on the long, worn counter that split the station into an office and interview room. On the opposite side, two desks formed islands between wooden and metal shelves on which folders and loose papers were stacked. The two desks were pushed together. A PC was mounted on one and on the other, papers, china cups and sandwich wrappers were piled up randomly, as if the occupant never had any free time. The room only had one window, and someone had put green-grey containers for files under the sill.

Übung 57: Was gehört zusammen? Ordnen Sie zu!

1. criminal	a) ☐ duty
2. police	b) ☐ appearance
3. jury	c) ☐ officer
4. crime	d) ☐ offence
5. victim	e) ☐ rate
6. court	f) ☐ support

Hunter and Percy simultaneously cleared their throats loudly and clearly, in an attempt to attract some attention. Horn immediately cleared his throat again when he heard Hunter do the same. It was his first mission; he didn't want to claim authority he didn't have.
A fleshy officer, unmistakably older, shuffled through the connecting door from the other room. His uniform could have done with washing, and it was too tight for him. It stretched over his voluminous stomach. A button was missing just above the navel. Greasy skin was visible underneath.
"You could get two Horns in those trousers," Hunter thought, mentally comparing the man with his assistant.
"Sir! We're looking for Sullivan," he said to the policeman. At first, the policeman replied with his sandwich wrapper. He dug around in it elaborately, rustling the wrapper loudly and extricated a final corner of bread. Feeling sick, the agents watched as he stuffed the remains of the bread and a large hunk of ham between his colourless lips. Sauce clung to the corner of his mouth. He pulled the sleeve of his shirt over his hand and rubbed the brown liquid off his chin. Only then did he turn to the visitors. He scrutinised them with dull eyes. He shuffled from the desk to the counter, laid one thick finger on the tabletop and said nothing.

ÜBUNG 58 !

*Übung 58: Äußern Sie Ihre Wünsche mit **I would like to**!*

1. you few ask a questions.

I would like to ask you a few questions.

2. been prepared have better.

3. happened what know.

4. able be you to help.

5. of the matter the truth to get.

"We're looking for Sullivan," repeated Hunter.

"And what do you want from him?" returned the man opposite. Up close, his eyes were no longer so dull, and Hunter thought he could detect a spark of recognition at the mention of Sullivan.

"You are Sullivan," he said quietly and professionally.

The other man gave nothing away. "And if I am, who wants to know?", he asked coolly.

"My name is Agent Hunter. This is my colleague Horn." The word colleague flattered Percy, and he moved closer behind his boss. Hunter went on, "Secret Service. Internal Affairs. I don't think I need to explain much. Sullivan, you were one of us, until the events with your wife and daughter."

The policeman didn't move. Hunter felt a sneaking suspicion that he had got the wrong person. He continued, “We’ve reopened the files, Sullivan, and it’s bloody obvious it wasn’t an accident. Have you got anything to say about it? Can you remember any details?”

Übung 59: Bilden Sie vollständige Aussage- oder Fragesätze!

ÜBUNG 59

1. we conduct investigation.

2. you know anything about the case?

3. you can help us with our investigations?

4. we look for new information on the case.

5. we think you know what happen.

6. you have anything to add?

As before, there was no reaction, so the agent carried on, “Your wife and the little one were found lying in the bathroom. Cause of death in the autopsy report was ‘Burning’. Cause of fire: ‘Accident. A pan left unattended on a gas ring in the kitchen’.

A bead of sweat wound its way from the policeman's left temple to his cheek. It dripped from his greyish face between his hands onto the wooden top of the counter. Hunter thought of Rosie and the invitation for dinner. "As soon as Ginny's out of the bath, I'll get started," Rosie had said. Hunter turned back to the man in front of him. "Sullivan, what mother bathes her small child and has food on the hob at the same time? What mother would leave the child in the water to go and quickly stir dinner?"

Sullivan nodded once, his thick lips opened. "I don't know what you're talking about."

Hunter was insistent. "Sullivan! Are you really Sullivan? Listen Sullivan. You can't help your family any more, that's clear. But you were once one of us, a British agent. As such, you know there are always corrupt elements in the Secret Service who'll sell us out. We should hold our heads above this kind of rotten stuff. Sullivan, who killed your family? Who put you under suspicion?"

Hunter's face was directly in front of the other man's. Another bead of sweat left a humid trail on Sullivan's cheek and split in two on a mole. One evaporated, the other dropped with a splash on the counter.

Übung 60: Welche Satzteile gehören zusammen?

1. Hunter kept asking questions although
2. Percy stayed quiet in spite of
3. The policeman refused to answer because
4. Hunter didn't get any answers despite
5. Secret agents can be corrupt even though
6. The policeman was sweating because of

a) ☐ his persistent questioning.
b) ☐ his desperation to ask some questions.
c) ☐ he didn't get any answers.
d) ☐ the tense atmosphere.
e) ☐ they are supposed to be honourable.
f) ☐ he didn't want to get involved.

"Sullivan, I'll get Miller for you. Help me." Hunter urged.
Deliberately the policeman turned around. His stomach brushed against the counter. He moved to the desk and picked up his empty sandwich wrapper. He balled it up in his massive fist. Listlessly, he tossed the ball towards the waste paper basket, but missed.

"We're closed.", he mumbled and motioned with an unmistakable nod towards the door. Then he shuffled back into the room he had come out of.
The two agents watched him at a loss. "Oh shit," cursed Hunter loudly.

Übung 61: Unterstreichen Sie die Verben!

ÜBUNG 61 !

A choking sound from the other room made him take notice. Hunter heard quiet steps, then a crack, and then a second, considerably louder crack. Hunter grabbed his weapon and rolled nimbly under the counter and out the other side. He ducked down and crept along to the dividing door; he glanced quickly from right to left and moved to the side of the counter opposite the door frame.
Hunter held his automatic pistol directly in front of him. He looked around to see if Horn was covering him from behind, but Percy had vanished.

"Well done," thought Hunter. He breathed in deeply and sprang into the frame of the open door. He swung the arm with the cocked pistol rapidly in both directions and took in the room with a quick look. A further door led into the yard It stood open. Sullivan lay strangely crumpled up on the floor. Blood was running from a wound on his head and sticking in his greasy hair. He must have injured himself falling against the edge of the table. Hunter followed the trail of blood from the piece of furniture.

The agent knelt down and felt the pulse in his neck. His finger became covered in the blood of the other man. Sullivan must have broken his neck. His head lay at a strange angle from his neck. The agent pulled himself to his feet. Directing a glance towards the open door, he placed both hands back on his weapon. He hurried to the door, checked round on all sides and stepped outside.

The yard was empty. A ramshackle bicycle leant against the wall which was surrounded by unkempt bushes. Hunter let his weapon fall. Shots rang out. They had to be coming from the front of the building. He sprinted back, swung past Sullivan's body, rolled under the counter and was on the street in front of the police station. Percy had taken cover behind his estate car and was firing wildly at a BMW which was roaring away on squealing tyres.

The occupant of the escaping car was firing back. Bullets bored through the metal of Hunter's car. When Hunter stepped out of the police station, he had to take cover. He threw himself to the asphalt and crawled forwards. A bullet skimmed just over his back and razed his skin. Pain burnt through him, but he just crouched lower. He had to get behind the car.

Percy fired again. If the car was out of reach, he wouldn't hear him.

"Percy!" thundered Hunter. "It's OK! You'd have to have a long range missile if you wanted to reach him!"

Übung 62: Welche Wörter gehören zusammen?

1. fracture	a) ☐ leg
2. graze	b) ☐ skin
3. cut	c) ☐ shoulder
4. break	d) ☐ bone
5. skin	e) ☐ finger
6. dislocate	f) ☐ knee

The young man sat down on the ground and stretched out his long legs. Without saying a word, he put his pistol, which he'd been tossing from hand to hand, back in its case. The older man leaned against the wheel next to him. Neither spoke for a while.

"It was worth a try," Hunter said finally.

"I want to hand in my notice," Percy said. His eyes stayed locked on the pistol. He took hold of the barrel with the outstretched fingers of his right hand; they swung like a pendulum in front of his face. "I left it in the car. Easy not to think about it." With these words he stretched out the weapon to Hunter.

"Your self-pity's mostly from nerves. Now pull yourself together. We've lost one of the most important pieces of information in this case. In fact, the most important. And now? Haven't you got a spark of honour left in your body? This is about the murder of a mother and her little child. A murderer from the ranks of the Secret Service. An organisation that you wanted to be in. And now, when this organisation isn't what it seems to be, you go off with your tail between your legs. Do you think that agents are born? You've got to work for it. Train, gain experience." Hunter broke off. He gesticulated wildly with his hands to back up what he was saying.

The expression on Percy's face changed from deep resignation and consternation to extreme anger.

"And if I hadn't left the police station, if I'd stayed there like you wanted, then no one would have seen Miller and his men. No one would have seen the bastard's getaway car. Maybe I didn't stop him, but at least I was there. Where were you anyway?"

In slow motion, Hunter changed his position and turned his body towards Percy. Very slowly he repeated, "Miller and his men?"

The other man confirmed it, "Yes, Miller and the two guys who kicked me out of the archives. I only saw Miller in the photo on the computer file. But I'm pretty sure it was him."

"You're a fine one." Hunter said nothing more. He gave him his hand and they both stood up. Hunter brushed the dirt from his jeans and checked that his leather jacket hadn't been damaged being dragged across the asphalt. Percy brushed himself off as well. He took a square metal box out of his pocket and checked it urgently. No, it didn't seem to be damaged from sitting on the hard ground.

"That had better not be what it looks like! If it is, then hopefully you didn't have it on?"

Hunter's objection amazed his assistant and he confirmed frankly, "My tracking device. So they know at HQ where we are in case anything happens. Service rule for outside missions: tracking device always ON."

ÜBUNG 63 !

Übung 63: Who is who with the Secret Service? Beantworten Sie die Fragen zum Text!

1. Hunter and Percy are ______________________________

2. Norma is ___________________________

3. Callaghan is ___________________________

4. Todd and Marvin are ______________________________

5. Sullivan was ______________________________

The evening with Rosie and her daughter did Hunter good. He forgot the day's incidents and relaxed. After Rosie had taken the protesting child to bed, she brought Hunter a coffee. They both sat for a while in Rosie's comfortable kitchen, stirring their drinks and passing the shortbread back and forth that was sitting in a metal tin on the table. Rosie had made the shortbread herself from her grandmother's recipe. Hunter took another biscuit from the tin and bit into it with enjoyment. A few crumbs fell from his lips onto the tablecloth. While he chewed happily, he brushed the crumbs to the floor with a swing of his outstretched hand.
The tablecloth was made of cream-coloured linen and perfectly matched the old-fashioned style kitchen with its wooden cupboards and numerous spice racks. On the hob, stood the remains of dinner in two silver pots. Hunter felt supremely content. Everything radiated cosiness. He was amazed at Rosie's talent of having something to say on every topic. "She'd make an outstanding undercover agent," he thought to himself.
Should he open up to her? He decided against it. He felt he needed people in his life who he could simply chat with.

Übung 64: Was gehört zusammen?

1. Could I have some more of the pie please?
2. Pass the salt please.
3. Do you like the soup?
4. Can I get you anything else?

5. Any one for seconds?
6. That was delicious, you're a great cook.

a) ☐ No thanks, I'm stuffed.
b) ☐ Of course, just help yourself.
c) ☐ It's great, thanks.
d) ☐ Thank you.
e) ☐ There you go.
f) ☐ Could I have some more wine please?

Back in his flat, Hunter felt his old zest returning – even stronger than this afternoon during the mission at the Pontypool police station. He knew he really only wanted one thing: to go back to working outside, back where the action was.
First, however, there were things to be solved. The story was far more complex than it had seemed. There must be more to it. He didn't trust Callaghan any further than he could throw her. And should he try to find out about Miller's colleagues?
He didn't know for sure how to proceed. But he wanted to string up this Miller and whoever his accomplices were. Who could kill a young child and her mother? He remembered the awful photos with the remains of the burnt corpses.

ÜBUNG 65 !

Übung 65: Welches Wort ist das „schwarze Schaf"?

1. police station, interview room, cell, surgery

2. culprit, accuser, criminal, burglar, offender

---

3. policeman, secret agent, spy, covert operation

---

4. machine gun, missile, arrow, pistol, revolver

Gina stood in front his bed. Her feminine body was covered by a soft night-dress made of see-through white chiffon. She wasn't wearing a bra. The night-dress reached to her hips and let the thin equally white lace suspender belt that lay round her waist shine through. From either side of the belt silk ribbons stretched down ending in small plastic clips. These clips almost disappeared in the white lace she had slipped them into. The lace border was just over four centimetres wide and wrapped round Gina's thigh. From the lace edging downward, her slim legs were wrapped in two extremely fine white stockings. Hunter's agent ran her hands over her body. Up and down and back up again. Pitch-black, softly curling hair fell to her shoulders. Her cheeks were red and on her face was a mixture of excited anticipation and impatience. He waited. She moved nearer, stretched both hands across the sheet. By doing this, she avoided touching his naked legs. She supported herself on her hands which she placed to the left and right of his body and crouched against the bed. She took her time. He stayed lying on his back and watched her. She wasn't wearing any lipstick. She straightened up in front of him.

ÜBUNG 66

Übung 66: Vervollständigen Sie die Sätze mit ***who, which*** *oder* ***that****!*

1. Gina was wearing a nightdress/was very sexy.

____

2. Hunter was very happy/they had some time together.

____

3. She was an agent/had very special talents.

____

4. They were on a mission/was top secret.

____

5. Hunter was a man/liked to work hard and play hard.

____

6. It was very important/they solve the case soon.

____

ÜBUNG 67

Übung 67: Setzen Sie die richtige Verbform ein!

Hunter screamed. He woke up and screamed again. He (1. can't bear) ________________ it. Where had that suddenly come from? All the blood? In her stomach a gaping hole, a crater. Hunter (2. jump out) ________________ of bed and ran into the bathroom. He turned on the tap and threw cold water on his face. More and more and more of it. He (3. be able to stop) ________________ for a long time. Finally he propped himself up on the edge of the washbasin and looked at himself in the mirror.

His brown hair looked almost black and stuck in wet strands to his forehead. His skin (4. be) ______ pale and bags bulged under his puffy eyes. After Gina's death in Italy, underlined by the fact that the mission had been a devastating failure, the dreams (5. start) ________. Sometimes it was a laughing Gina in a gondola on the canals of Venice. Sometimes it was a sad and exhausted Gina in his arms after one of the cinema performances. Gina, in the light of a candle in a much too expensive restaurant (6. hold) ______ the end of a piece of spaghetti in her mouth, as he (7. chew) ______ on the other end. Gina, sucking up noodles and giggling when some sauce spilt on the damask tablecloth and quickly putting the bottle of basalmic vinegar over the dirty spot. His Gina; and then always the blood from the stomach. In the last few months the dreams had grown less frequent. But they (8. not stop) ____________.

"Maybe Callaghan's right. Maybe it did break me." thought Hunter. He stared unremittingly at his face in the mirror. "Falling in love with a colleague in the Italian Secret Service while on an international mission. Colleague dies during the mission. Agent needs psychiatric treatment. Agent refuses it. Agent makes careless mistakes. Agent needs psychiatric treatment. Agent needs a holiday. Agent needs to be transferred to internal service."

He stopped the flow of his thoughts. His eyes narrowed. He felt the energy of the past day return. He saw Rosi and Ginny at the dinner table. He saw Sullivan, grey and dulled by desk service.

He tightened his grip on the washbasin. He pushed his shoulders back and pulled his body upright. Then he raised his head.

"Callaghan, you're not going to crush me. Agent Hunter is back."

With a quick movement, he reached for the towel that hung next to the washbasin. He dried his hands and face as he hurried back into the bedroom from the bathroom. He flung the towel carelessly on the bed and opened his wardrobe. He rummaged between the hangers. Soon he had the photo of Gina in nothing but her white chiffon in front of him. Absentmindedly he said, "Go darling. I'll always love you." His hand touched the rubbery material of his 'mission suit'. He took the hanger from the rail and pulled the suit from the cupboard. He held it up at arm's length and felt the material. A second later he threw it hastily on the bed next to the towel and dug in the bottom of the cupboard for the accompanying boots.

ÜBUNG 68 !

Übung 68: Beantworten Sie die Fragen in ganzen Sätzen mit einer Verneinung!

1. Do you think Sullivan's family died by accident?

____

2. Do they have enough evidence yet to prove who killed Sullivan's family?

____

3. Is Hunter finished as an active agent?

4. Do you think Callaghan is involved in the mystery?

5. Is Percy useless as a secret agent?

Hunter casually slung his blue rucksack on the floor next to his desk, swung a leg onto the seat of his chair, sat down and leaned his back comfortably against the chair. He stretched his legs out on the table. He looked at his muscular calves in blue jeans with satisfaction. He shook his mission boots, which he'd chosen to wear instead of his trainers.

He felt like he had when he was in external service, when he went to work everyday in these black boots with thick rubber soles.

Now he noticed the absence of his young colleague. Percy had been in the office before him the entire week. Today though, his ball lay alone and forgotten under the desk and the PC was off.

Hunter crossed his arms behind his head. A childlike anticipation filled him. He was so close to cracking this case. He was sure of it. What he didn't have was a plan.

Norma broke into his thoughts. The psychologist hurried through the open office door and looked at him distractedly. Hunter didn't even have time to greet her before she disappeared again. A few seconds later she was standing in the door again, this time she turned directly to the agent.

"Sorry I didn't mean to be rude. I didn't want to ignore you."

ÜBUNG 69

Übung 69: Bitten Sie um etwas mehr Klarheit!

1. tell me exactly what happened

Could you tell me exactly what happened?

2. clear up some confusion

___

3. help us with our enquiries

___

4. explain how events unfolded

___

5. tell us why you were there in the first place

___

With these words, she stepped into the room and headed for Hunter's desk. Suddenly, she stopped. Her grey hair was especially tousled today and the jacket of her suit was open, as were the top two buttons of her blouse. She held her throat with one hand as if she wasn't sure she was getting enough air and was being stifled. A torrent of words came down at Hunter.

"I can tell you. You know her. I've had enough. Since that cow replaced McCarthy the entire place has been turned upside down. Tell me what good has come of this?" Hunter was convinced he really shouldn't give any advice. Dumbly he waited for a pause in the older woman's diatribe. She continued her tirade.

"She wants to submit decisions on redundancies and transfers to me and I have to give them my blessing with my signature. Saying that in the psychologist's opinion, colleagues are incompetent or burned out, so it's easier for her to back up her capricious personnel decisions." Norma's fist worked the tabletop. Hunter's leg took the vibrations and he hurried to get her to move from the table.

"I don't get the chance to see these people that she wants to get rid of. She thinks she's a doctor and that she's competent enough for these assessments." Norma wheezed, "Ask yourself what kind of doctor she is. Do you know?"

This time the pause lasted longer and Hunter felt a response was required.

"No, not a clue. Criminology? Political Science?"

Norma waved these away with a dismissive hand gesture. "I don't know either and I don't care. She's not going to mess up my job any more. I explained it to the youngsters a few years ago. She was a trainee then in external service and was taking orders from Captain Montgomery. I could tell you something there. Her and her fine partner on a mission in Madrid. Do you know, Spain is my …"

Übung 70: Welche Erklärung stimmt?

1. "Over my dead body!"
   a) ☐ It won't happen if I can stop it.
   b) ☐ I will die if that happens.

2. "I'm all ears!"
   a) ☐ I eavesdrop on people all the time.
   b) ☐ I'm ready to listen to you.

3. "What are you getting at?"
   a) ☐ What are you bringing to the meeting?
   b) ☐ What do you mean?

4. “I wasn’t born yesterday!”
   a) ☐ I knew about it before you.
   b) ☐ I’m not stupid.

5. “That’s more like it!”
   a) ☐ It’s better than before.
   b) ☐ It’s worse than before.

6. “It’s all go here!”
   a) ☐ It’s very busy.
   b) ☐ Everyone has gone out.

Here the psychologist’s tirade was interrupted by a knocking sound. Nelson Peterson knocked on the doorframe again.
“The door was open,” he apologised. “To be honest, I’ve been standing here for a while.”
Under pale brows, his blue eyes were directed uncertainly at Norma. Their eyes met then his gaze flitted away. Hunter also glanced at the psychologist to see if she wanted to finish her story or break it off. Norma went for the latter.
“That’s done me good. Thanks for listening. I feel better now.”

She made a show of offering Hunter her hand. Then she turned, nodded shortly to Peterson and began to do up her jacket as she left. Peterson was apparently looking for somewhere to sit, and stood undecided in the doorway, not knowing quite where to put himself. Hunter motioned with a pen to Percy’s desk and indicated to Peterson that he could sit on the ball. While Peterson was struggling to bring the ball out from behind the desk in the narrow office space, the agent carried on drawing on the notepad that lay in front of him. His pen circled the names ‘Callaghan’ and ‘Montgomery’. A line joined the two circles and he began to draw another empty circle. In capital letters was the name 'Miller'.

*Übung 71: **As** oder **when**? Unterstreichen Sie!*

ÜBUNG 71 !

1. As/When I was training, I met Callaghan for the first time.
2. As/When the suspect was arrested he tried to escape.
3. As/When we were talking, we didn't hear the knocking.
4. As/When I was twenty, I started training as a secret agent.
5. As/When I tried to open the safe, the alarm went off.

Peterson gave up trying to free the ball from under the table and sat without further ado on Percy's desk. He moved some papers to the side, turned the pear picture frame round and put it disconcertedly back where it belonged. Hunter was worried about Peterson's report. Following a spontaneous decision, he had taken him the photos from Miller's file two days ago. Instead of presenting the results of his investigation, Nelson started with a question.
"Who actually were the woman and girl in the pictures?" Hunter had almost seen it coming. That was another reason why many people didn't welcome or avoided working with Peterson. He confused himself. He didn't deliver the basic specialist report. He wanted to know what it was about and, where possible, solve it himself. It was better to keep quiet or it could take weeks or months to get an analysis from him. However, he could afford to be eccentric. He was the best in his field.
To try and get round this, Hunter had sent a short summary to the lab. When he took the photos to Peterson, he had explained it was about the murder of a colleague's family and he hoped to reopen an old and lapsed case.

It was not the aspects of the case such as uncovering an injustice, that inspired the pathologist in his investigations. It was the thought of discovering something that another investigator had overlooked or falsely interpreted.

ÜBUNG 72 !

Übung 72: Bilden Sie vollständige Fragesätze!

1. The accident happened years ago.

The accident happened years ago, didn't it?

2. They were an agent's wife and daughter.

____

3. It seems a bit suspicious.

____

4. Something has been covered up.

____

5. It can be solved.

____

"It's obvious to me that a mother doesn't leave something on the hob and bathe her child at the same time. The mother would have to go and stir the food occasionally and leave the child unattended. Apart from that, the way the body is lying is similar to another case that Miller was on when he was younger."
Peterson furrowed his brow and signalled to Hunter that he needed further explanation.

“It’s all a bit vague. Miller was only the officer who did the investigation in the first case. In the second, he was the Captain responsible. And the way Todd took the blame for this ‘accident’ so quickly, seems really strange to me. Also, that the boss is going to the bother of keeping it absolutely quiet. And then these guys in the archive who beat up my associate, who are again connected to Miller.”

Peterson stopped rolling about on the ball. Attentively he listened for the agent’s explanation. He was used to looking for needles in haystacks in his profession. Minute particles of skin often brought the cleverest cover-ups and the most experienced burglars before the court through DNA testing.

“I’m still collecting incidents,” Hunter explained referring to his list of various bullet points. He would have preferred it if the pathologist had presented a well thought out theory. He reported on the results of the previous day at the small town police station. Peterson clicked his tongue as Hunter finished.

“Of course,” he said, “My esteemed colleague had his tracking device on the whole time. Meaning, anyone who wanted to know where you were, knew.”

Peterson was annoyed.

“Did I forget to say that we were skiving off and researching on our own initiative.” Hunter put in casually.

Peterson laughed out loud. “Not bad!” he cheered, “That’s what I call bravery!”

Übung 73: Bringen Sie die Sätze in die richtige Reihenfolge!

1. exhibit court I A the present to.

____

ÜBUNG 73 !

2. witness to call number stand the I eight.

____

3. the you swear truth to whole do tell?

____

4. court order in!

____

5. questions you further have do any?

____

Hunter wasn't sure if he was serious or joking. He spontaneously decided to go for a broad grin. He seemed to have guessed Peterson's intentions correctly.

"Finally someone here is taking something into their own hands," Peterson confirmed his pleasure once more. He was still for a moment and appeared to be looking for the right words with which to begin.

"Hunter," he said turning to him, "You're hunched over a pile of clues and yet you don't know anything."

With a hand gesture he warded off any objections against this conclusion. Hunter shut his mouth again.

"If I tell you that the woman in the photo definitely didn't die in a fire, but must have already been dead, don't just throw it on the pile of evidence. Start with that. Analysis of the pictures on the PC showed that you're right. She was shot from behind. It looks a lot like a 'Macster 47' to me. It's just a suspicion; we'd need the remains of the bullet or skin samples from the entry hole. I've asked about it; nothing was saved. If it was even collected properly.

Unfortunately, the only part of the child's body visible is the part hanging out of the bath. I don't know about anything above the throat. If she was shot, it must have been in the neck or head."
The ease with which the pathologist referred to these things shocked the agent every time, despite his years of experience.

Übung 74: Vervollständigen Sie die Sätze mit ***still*** *oder* ***already****!*

1. We haven't got enough evidence.

We still haven't got enough evidence.

2. We know a lot about what happened that night.

3. Callaghan is getting suspicious.

4. Do you want to get involved?

5. There's a lot of work to do.

"And I'll tell you something else. What this Miller as commanding officer wrote on the death certificates is a joke. Anybody else would have done a proper investigation here. Although, under Captain Montgomery, strange things always happen. Not that I've got anything against His Eminence.
At the mention of Miller, Hunter broke in, "What do you know about Montgomery?" he asked hastily.

Peterson pointed at his chest. "Old man, who's been in the service longer? I was a kid in the eighties. You were maybe lightly greying then. That's why I'll give you a few clues – Perms, cowboy boots, and clothes with sequins all over. The girls all had these flowered bodysuits that fastened between the legs with snaps."

Hunter felt himself slipping away from the conversation.

"You don't remember anything about Montgomery?" Nelson brought him back.

"Register this. Then I was just a beginner in pathology and wasn't allowed to speak to the great Montgomery. But from hearsay, the name means something to me." Peterson defended himself.

At this moment, Hunter realised why he was the agent and not this man's partner. Hunter stuck to facts, not hearsay. Peterson interrupted his thoughts.

"In your position I would rely on the facts."

Hunter was caught startled and heard the other man say, "The needle in your haystack is so big that it would prick even a blind person. How often do you want to connect a piece of evidence with Miller's name and then just put it on the pile with the rest of your clues?"

The obviousness of this train of thought astounded Hunter and he knew what the conclusion would be even before Peterson could finish.

"Just ask this Miller person."

ÜBUNG 75 !

Übung 75: Ordnen Sie richtig zu!

a) filing cabinet b) to work undercover c) to wash the dishes d) colleague e) armchair f) client g) concealed weapon h) to

raid i) to relax j) canteen k) double agents l) guests m) bed
n) spies o) receptionist

1. On a mission

___

2. In the office

___

3. At home

___

Hunter slid his tray along the serving counter. He wanted to have a quick late lunch in the canteen to build up his strength for the questioning. Peterson's idea of questioning Miller was simple and at the same time inspired. As the head of 'Internal Affairs', it had been easy for Hunter to invite the Captain for a meeting that very afternoon. The experienced agent hadn't said anything about it being an 'inquisition'. He had also let Captain Miller believe that it was about the two men in his unit, Todd and Marvin, who had been involved in the 'accident' with the witness.
"Are you only having an apple?" Percy disturbed Hunter's thoughts. On his own tray balanced a portion of Shepherd's Pie with gleaming green mint sauce and a slab of pink coloured blancmange, crowned with a cocktail cherry. A cup of coffee and a glass of orange juice rounded off the meal.
"I'm going to grab a sandwich," Hunter answered and turned to the glass cabinets where sandwiches and other cold meals were displayed.

Übung 76: Beim Essen: Welche Wörter gehören zusammen?

1. Macaroni	a) ☐ stew
2. Toad in the	b) ☐ cheese
3. Welsh	c) ☐ pudding
4. Lancashire	d) ☐ rarebit
5. Irish	e) ☐ hole
6. Yorkshire	f) ☐ hotpot

Percy waited for him at the cashdesk. Apparently he was upset by the fact that he had spent the morning in the underground at Victoria Station and had arrived late at the office. He was paying his boss even more attention than was normally the case. Above all, since he had heard that they were to undertake an 'inquisition', there was no stopping him. Hunter saw from his expression that he had even more questions.

"Percy, the most important thing is to go in there strongly," Hunter warded him off.

When you're eating, you can't talk, thought Hunter to himself. He would soon realise how wrong he was.

*Übung 77: Vervollständigen Sie die Sätze mit **for** oder **since**!*

1. Percy waited at the station/a long time.

____

2. They have been investigating the case/the beginning of the week.

____

3. Hunter hadn't eaten/breakfast.

____

4. The case had been allowed to lapse/several years.

____

5. Callaghan has been the boss/five days.

____

6. Montgomery has been retired/1997.

____

Übung 78: Setzen Sie die passenden Wörter in die Lücken ein! ***(deciding, silvery, expectant, sure, bags, drove, possible, grilling)***

He was 1. __________ of himself as he sat there in front of Hunter, body leaning back in a relaxed position, waiting. From the ceiling, the neon light shone on Miller's hair, which was run through with fine strands of grey. It gave his thick, blond curls an almost 2. ________________ shimmer. It didn't really go with his round, red face. Or with the tiredness Hunter could see in his guest's eyes. Perhaps Miller wasn't so self-confident and relaxed, it was 3. _________________ he had just gone to bed too late. Hunter didn't let himself worry about this for long.

ÜBUNG 78 !

“He’s got 4. ________________ under his eyes you could kick a football into.” The thought amused Hunter. He decided not to give Miller a 5. _____________________. He would just bring out the accusation.

With a loud sniff, Percy raised his nose high. The young man 6. _____________ Hunter crazy.

Percy looked at the man sitting in front of him with 7. _________________ eyes. It was his first real ‘inquisition’. Not just a role-play, like he’d had to do in his training. This was real life. Percy was excited about the first question Hunter would direct at Miller. Therein lay the trick, he had learnt. The first question was the 8. ________________ one.

The young man had eagerly brought a pen and paper to take personal notes on Hunter’s strategy and laid it on the table in from of him. Hunter’s gaze wandered to his young colleague and back to Miller. He was still leaning back in his chair with his arms folded. With the palm of his hand, Hunter leant on the table that stood between him and his visitor. The first question. An arrogant grin widened on the experienced agent’s face. He raised his left eyebrow and scrutinised Miller. How to begin? Hunter decided spontaneously on the tactic of isolation. He would tentatively use apparently inconsequential questions. He would lull the accused into a false sense of security and then at the right moment …

Übung 79: Befragen Sie Miller!

1. Where you night of October 12th?

Where were you on the night of October the 12th?

2. When last see Mike Sullivan?

___

3. Present night the witness died?

___

4. What movements October 11th?

___

5. Have an alibi night of June 20th?

___

Percy let out a loud snort. He lifted up his nose once again and snorted once more. Then he slid his chair round and fixed Hunter with a cheerful look. Hunter swallowed audibly.

"Mr Miller, where were you on the night of the 12th and 13th October 1995?"

Miller's eyes narrowed. "We're not in the police here. I'm being held here against my will. I want to speak to my lawyer." Miller spoke calmly and assuredly.

Only a small twitch of his eyes gave away any sign of strain. Hunter thought of the football and the bags under his eyes again.

"Of course, Miller. No one knows you're here. Therefore no one's going to come looking for you. Perhaps you'd like to work with us and tell us where you were on the night in question. It would be easier for all involved and would save you and us a lot of time."

Hunter heard another snort from Percy and continued, "Well Miller, on that night you were on duty here and at ten o'clock you left HQ." With that, he hit the palm of his hand on a sheet of paper which had tables with rows of numbers and dates printed on it. He laid the sheet back on the top of the file that lay in front of him. Miller waited.

Übung 80: Was machen die Personen gerade? Vervollständigen Sie die Sätze mit der richtigen Zeitform des Verbs!

1. (Right now) (to try to control himself) (Miller)

___

2. (Currently) (Percy) (to watch the interview excitedly)

___

3. (At this moment) (Miller) (to begin to sweat)

___

4. (At the moment) (to give Miller a grilling) (Hunter)

___

5. (Percy) (to learn a lot) (right now)

___

6. (Hunter) (currently) (to feel powerful)

___

"You left land and travelled by water. You knew where Sullivan was on holiday with his family. You also knew that that night, Sullivan would be called on a special mission. You had arranged it yourself

during your shift in the office." Miller's gaze became fixed. He stared at the tabletop between Hunter and himself.
Percy sneezed. Hunter hunted in his pocket for a pack of tissues and slapped them onto the table gruffly. His palm stayed on the pack. "Thanks boss," said Percy and, "Sorry."
Startled, Miller had removed his gaze from the table. His self-assurance had returned.

"Now I've got you!," thought Hunter. He looked Miller directly in the eye, his nostrils flaring. A finger on his left hand curled itself round the pack of tissues. With a threatening stare Hunter went on, "You killed the wife and girl. Then you set the house on fire. During the investigation, you pointed the finger at Sullivan and told everyone that he murdered his family. You bastard!"
Miller started. The volume and suddenness of the words had hit him with the force of a blow. The room was deathly silent. Only the crackling of the neon lights could be heard. Rhythmic, like the ticking of a clock.
Miler turned to Hunter's face. He began quietly, "I wanted …"
'Crack'. Hunter and Miller both started at the same time. Percy was laying down what was left of his broken pen. He shrugged his shoulders quickly, folded his notebook shut and laid the two halves of the pen on the table.

Übung 81: Finden Sie ein weiteres Substantiv!

1. investigation — *investigator*
2. detection — ____________
3. administrator — ____________

4. crime ____________

5. suspicion ____________

6. operator ____________

At the same moment the door of the 'inquisition' room opened with a jerk. Callaghan stood on the threshold, hands on her hips. The skirt of her severely cut suit had slid up a little, exposing a knee, which was pointing sharply forward.

"Hunter what's going on here? Break this up right now!"

Under the backcombed pageboy cut, her eyes blazed. Her expression was stiff under the hair which had been shaped with much effort and hairspray.

"Does she at least take off the helmet to sleep?" wondered Hunter.

After his boss had left, Hunter stretched his limbs. He wanted clarity. He turned on his PC and went through her files in the digital databank. As he had suspected – the files were no longer there, just a perfect glossy CV. A typical career in the Secret Service, perhaps with a bit more distinction and faster advancement than most. The rapid rise to the highest position in the Secret Service had been sponsored by a head honcho from the House of Commons. It seemed quite a few members of government had nothing but praise for Callaghan. This wasn't really anything unusual for the head of a state Secret Service.

"Should I send Percy back down to the archive files in the cellar?" thought Hunter idly.

That would all take too long. Today he wanted to do the job properly. Hunter knew his boss to be a pedantic person. He was pretty sure that above everything, she followed each and every protocol exactly. And, given the time, she was able to fall back on factual information: to get rid of a tiresome colleague or to make the career path easier for her new pet. His plan was simple and met with the so-called 'Basic Knowledge' every agent had: sneak up, hunt, take, leave.

*Übung 82: Beschreiben Sie Hunters Pläne! Benutzen Sie **going to**!*

ÜBUNG 82

1. (find the files on Miller)

____

2. (get justice for Sullivan and his family)

____

3. (expose Callaghan as a fraud)

____

4. (restore his reputation as an agent)

____

5. (make Percy admire him)

____

6. (get back out of the office)

____

As he entered the Secret Service building at eleven o'clock, Wayne looked at him questioningly from the lobby. Hunter told the night watchman all about doing overtime for an very big and tricky case. It wasn't the first time he's lied.

In his office on the seventh floor, he removed his street clothes and then checked each piece carefully before he laid it down. It had only been two weeks since he had used his 'mission suit'. He had

installed a software programme on his computer that would surf the internet randomly for the next few hours. His alibi was taken care of if anyone asked about his night visit to the building. Hopefully the software wouldn't visit too many sites with dodgy contents. How embarrassing that would be!
He stretched himself into his tight, black 'mission suit'. The smooth, latex material fitted his body perfectly. His muscles bulged out from under it. To his disappointment, you could also see the edges of his boxer shorts and T-shirt that he was wearing underneath. He'd put on extra thin underclothes because of it.
The suit had a hood which Hunter carefully pushed his hair into. The more aerodynamic his body was, the better. For this reason, the suit was also fitted out with an integrated system that was water repellent and let sweat through at regular intervals. This kept the material elastic and supple. His black gloves were made of the same material. His feet went into his mission boots with the thick rubber soles. In the soles there were extendable soles, for the winter, treads for difficult terrain and rubber nodules. Hunter had decided on the rubber nodules. They dampened sound when he was moving and prevented his steps from causing vibrations on the floor.

ÜBUNG 83 !

Übung 83: Welches ist das passende Synonym? Ordnen Sie zu!

1. stealth	a) ☐ awareness
2. caution	b) ☐ slyness
3. alertness	c) ☐ hush
4. silence	d) ☐ carefulness

He looked at his watch. Five past twelve. He left his office and took the lift to the top floor. On arriving, he slid along the corridor in the dark. No one would be working on this floor so late.

Determinedly he neared the heavy oak door of Callaghan's office. The wood shimmered a spooky green through the glass of his tinted glasses, on which he'd activated the nightvision function. There were far too many video cameras in this part of the building. The assigned guards for the night patrols seldom kept to a minute by minute patrol. If Hunter was lucky the guards would be paying attention to outside security and implementing the previous casual internal system.

"We want to make things as friendly as possible here," his previous boss, McCarthy, was always saying. Up to now, no one had managed to infiltrate the Secret Service from outside. It was almost impossible. There was no fear of anyone getting through the security checks, due to the body scan, the voice recognition, the DNA check and the night watchmen in the lobby. For Hunter as an employee, these were of course not a problem.

Übung 84: Was ist richtig, ***when*** *oder* ***if****? Unterstreichen Sie!*

ÜBUNG 84 !

1. When/If Hunter gets into Callaghan's office he will look for the files.
2. When/If the files are in the office, Hunter will find them.
3. When/If Hunter tells Percy tomorrow he will be very impressed.
4. When/If they have the files they can accuse Miller.
5. When/If he is successful, Hunter will be very pleased.

The agent fiddled in the brass lock of the door with a needle. A quiet click told him the lock had opened. He removed his ear from the wood of the door and pushed the handle slowly and carefully down with his gloved hand. Callaghan was known for her knowledge of each and every security trick. She would have taken precautions. Hunter was sure of this. The general Secret Service philosophy: 'We protect ourselves from enemies and trust our own', was meaningless for a woman of her calibre. In general, she upheld the formula. Hunter could regrettably vouch for this. A muted hiss signalled to him that opening the door had set off some kind of mechanism. He switched his glasses to normal sight. From his position in the doorframe he could see that thin laser beams crossed the room. They were diagonal, vertical and horizontal and built up a dense net. He ventured forward only far enough to allow the door to shut behind him. He breathed in and thought. Then he sank soundlessly onto all fours. He adroitly wound his way through the triangle that the direct routes of the laser beams had left free above the floor. Just behind him, a horizontal light beam blocked another beam a few millimetres above the parquet. The polished wooden floor didn't make the exercise any easier. The surface of his suit seemed to glitter like ice. His fingers already hurt. It felt like an enormous effort to control his slippery body with just the suckers on his gloves.

ÜBUNG 85 !

Übung 85: Welche Ereignisse sind zum Zeitpunkt der Handlung schon passiert?

1. ☐ Percy drove Hunter's car.
2. ☐ They collected lots of new information.
3. ☐ Hunter was beaten up.
4. ☐ Callaghan fired Norma.
5. ☐ Hunter's girlfriend died.
6. ☐ Percy graduated from the Academy.
7. ☐ Callaghan became the boss.

8. ☐ Percy solved the case.
9. ☐ Norma got very upset.
10. ☐ Hunter moved to a new office.

He had to bend his neck slightly backwards to go forwards without putting himself in danger. As he was doing, this he looked directly into the lens of a camera that was hanging vertically from the ceiling. It was almost perfectly integrated into the beams of the wooden ceiling. There, directly under it in the shallow light of the laser beams, he could see the metal ring that bordered the lens.

Staying in his twisted position he fumbled around on his belt for his catapult. It was worth its weight in gold several times over. In fact, it was just a rubberband attached to pieces of leather. He put the leather into his mouth and loaded the rubber band. Then he stretched the rubber over his thumb and forefinger and pulled with his ring finger. It was practical. One hand was enough for this simple utensil. His forefinger let the band go.

Nothing happened. Hunter twirled the rubber that seemed to have stuck itself fast to the leather. The second shot was lucky. The weight flew through the air and met the eye of the camera with a crash. A minute piece of the lens was left, but Hunter wasn't worried about that. He peered around for other cameras.
"Nothing?" he whispered. On Callaghan's desk, which was opposite him, a forgotten sandwich missing its crusts and an apple which had been bitten into were mouldering. A laser beam burnt into the apple and another one into a paper napkin which half covered the bread. No roasting, no ashes, no explosion. He had been taken in by her.

ÜBUNG 86 !

Übung 86: Welche Wörter gehören zusammen?

1. catapult	a) ☐ arrow
2. pistol	b) ☐ cannonball
3. bow	c) ☐ bullets
4. sword	d) ☐ stone
5. cannon	e) ☐ shield

Briskly he righted himself and cut through more laser beams. Nothing happened. He carefully stepped up to her desk. His eyes took in the ceiling and the walls. That couldn't be everything that Callaghan had managed to muster. He had thought briefly of bringing his metal detector on the mission to trace the metal parts of other cameras. He didn't really know if the ring round the lens wasn't just made of silver plastic. Others were full of chromed furnishings instead of metal parts.

He decided to go for the direct way. He would deal with the cupboards and shelves afterwards. Now he wanted to take a closer look at her desk. Above the leather chair, hung a framed pop art picture. The Campbell's tin of beans by Andy Warhol. He doubted it was genuine. Warhol was one of the few artists Hunter liked. Perhaps because he was one of the few whose paintings he could immediately tell apart from other artists.

In McCarthy's time, in the place of the Warhol hung an etching of London in Shakespearean times. In the entrance to one of the Bankside dives depicted therein was an old-fashioned combination lock. This released a mechanism and the picture swung forward from the left on hinges and opened like a door. McCarthy had handed out advice from under it.

"Refreshments for the war council", as he had called it. A hiding place was clichéd and used in every gangster film. That's why

McCarthy was even more pleased to have a hidden safe. Normally it was home to his spirits. Hunter had only once been shown the hiding place during a social get-together.

Übung 87: Wählen Sie die höflichste Antwort!

ÜBUNG 87 !

1. "Thank you so much for inviting me."
   a) ☐ Not at all.
   b) ☐ My wife made me.

2. "You've gone to so much effort."
   a) ☐ Oh, it's nothing.
   b) ☐ No, I haven't.

3. "Oh no, I've spilt some wine!"
   a) ☐ How stupid.
   b) ☐ It doesn't matter.

4. "This wine is wonderful."
   a) ☐ Glad you think so.
   b) ☐ I don't like it.

The agent doubted Callaghan would use such a trivial hiding place, especially for secret documents or the like. But perhaps she also had a similar weakness for long used secret devices like her predecessor. And he had to begin his search somewhere.
He rounded the corner of her desk. He just wanted to move the chair to the side so he could stand in front of the picture.
A piercing pain in his left upper arm made him start. He staggered backwards.

He put his right hand on the place where it hurt. The wound wasn't big, but it was bleeding a lot. At the same time, his gaze swept the floor. One shone out between all the laser beams that crossed the room. He must have walked into a type of photoelectric barrier between the leg of Callaghan's desk and the wall. Hunter wanted to step over the light beam. When he had his leg directly above the pale line pain ran through him again. Now somewhat higher in his left shoulder. This time a dart was stuck in it. He guessed he had moved no more than ten centimetres and he must have been shot from somewhere to the side. Hunter stepped back behind the light beam. He touched the missile with trembling fingers. Renewed pain ran through his body. He gritted his teeth. With a jerk, he pulled the arrow out of the gaping wound. Some flesh and skin hung from it. Hunter looked at the arrow in his hand.

ÜBUNG 88 !

Übung 88: Unterstreichen Sie die richtige Alternative!

1. The wound on Hunter's shoulder hurt the most/mostest.
2. Callaghan had used the trivialest/most trivial hiding place.
3. Hunter had the fastest/most fast reaction time of any agent.
4. Callaghan's office was the dangerousest/most dangerous place in the building.
5. Percy was the tallest/most tall agent Hunter had ever seen.
6. Hunter was still one of the fittest/most fit agents in the Secret Service.

The mechanism that had attacked him this time when he wanted to get closer to the back of the desk was clear. It involved a wall of light that stretched above the pale beams. He wanted to come into contact with it once more. Two arrows would be enough.

A slim middle section was lined by two plastic pieces as 'feathers' behind and a strong aerodynamic point. They worked as darts. Hunter shuddered as he looked once more at the point of the arrow. The piece of flesh that hung on the barb was rosy. There was a hole in his uniform.

The agent completed the standard procedure when faced with such a weapon. From the underarm of his sleeve he folded out an integrated, flat aluminium case, pressed the point of the arrow into a light blue piece of felt and instantly a red digital signal was flashing, which quickly showed sequences of different number and letter codes. After a few seconds, it turned green and gave a breakdown of the materials.

Hunter folded the aluminium case shut. He was only interested in the first check for poisonous substances. Some controversy with jungle tribes in the course of his career had taught him to be careful with arrows.

*Übung 89: Bilden Sie **If-Sätze**!*

ÜBUNG 89 !

1. Hunter was more careful. He avoided the dart.

If Hunter had been more careful, he would have avoided the dart.

2. Hunter was better prepared. He brought his metal detector.

____

3. Callaghan had lots of defences. It was more difficult.

____

4. He knew what he was looking for. He was more focussed.

____

5. Percy was less clumsy. He brought him too.

____

6. He had some concrete evidence. He didn't need to be here.

____

He started. Outside in the corridor, voices were coming closer. Where could he disappear to quickly? The voices came up to the door. Panicking, he looked around. The top of the desk was made of smoked glass.
"I'd be recognised underneath," he thought. Should he hide behind the cupboard or behind one of the two sets of shelves?
"Up obviously!"

! ÜBUNG 90

Übung 90: Setzen Sie die richtige Verbform in die Lücke ein! Achten Sie auf die richtigen Zeiten!

He jumped through the wall of light. The arrow which (1. to release) ____________________ shot through the air. Hunter ducked. The shot missed him by a hair's breadth. The agent rolled over and (2. to slide) __________________ behind the massive leather chair that stood behind the desk.
A key turned in the lock. The handle moved down a few times. The key moved in the lock again. This time the door (3. to spring) _____________ open and (4. to open) ________________ outwards.

Obviously there was a connection between the lock mechanism and the laser beams. The last ones suddenly disappeared.

"It'll just (5. to take) ______________ a minute Shawn. Without my mobile I'm half a woman," Hunter (6. to hear) ____________ from his hiding place. It was Callaghan's unpleasant, piercing tone. His boss came up to the desk. The man (7. to accompany) ___________ her could be heard from behind.

"No problem sweetheart. Now I get (8. to see) _______________ where you 'get busy'.

At the word 'sweetheart' Hunter started. His stomach began to churn and he felt a chuckle rising. "Don't laugh. Don't laugh," he thought and forced himself to be quiet.
"Come in quickly and shut the door. Then no one will see you in here," admonished the woman. From his hiding place Hunter could make out her legs in the pumps that were too high. He held his breath.
"Don't move," he ordered himself.
Now another pair of legs in dark leather shoes were there.
"Why?" said a male voice, "It doesn't matter if anyone sees us sweetheart." The chuckle rose in Hunter's throat again. He began to count slowly to take his mind off it.
"Do you want me to get you another battery charger for Christmas? Then you could keep this one and still forget the other one."
The voice had become high and flattering.
"Please don't start …" begged Hunter. At that moment he heard a sound like two bodies tumbling on to the leather sofa. He could see

nothing more than a pair of leather shoes hovering in the air and two pumps which fell to the floor, one after the other.

Übung 91: Welche Wörter sind Kosenamen? Kreuzen Sie an!

1. ☐ dearest
2. ☐ sweetie pie
3. ☐ moron
4. ☐ lovey
5. ☐ dopey
6. ☐ darling

Hunter's leg tingled. It had gone to sleep. He had to get rid of the tingling. He had to think of a plan. What should he do?
A horrified cry made him jump. He was almost upright. His heart skipped a beat. He silently let his breath out through his mouth.
"Hold on!" he encouraged himself. He ignored the tingling in his calf. He stayed bravely in his uncomfortable position.
The two lovebirds got up from the sofa. The agent heard a astonished 'Sweetheart' that the man uncertainly hissed between his teeth. In the meantime, Hunter had got used to the word. The chuckle stayed in his throat.
"Miller, put your weapon away, you idiot. What's all this nonsense?" Callaghan's sentence cut through the silence like the lash of a whip. The man accompanying her was struck dumb.
"What do you want?" she continued.
Miller's voice sounded stronger and more threatening than it had a few hours ago in their interview.
"Helene, I've had enough! What are you trying to pull here? What does this Hunter want from me and why is he digging around in the stuff about Sullivan?"

Callaghan tried to move the conversation in a less aggressive direction. Quietly she said, "Listen Stan. Now put your weapon down, and we'll talk to each other like normal people."
"Since when have I been a normal man, Helene? You're career crazed too. You're career crazed in the extreme!"
Callaghan cut him off, "You sissy! You've never stepped out of line. And in case you hadn't noticed, I'm always there to save your ass."
"I can save my own ass. Listen, Helene …"
"What are you really doing creeping around here? In the middle of the night?"
"I want the files, Helene. I don't think these files should exist. I was always against not destroying them. I'm here to get them. How handy that we met. Now I don't have to spend ages looking. Give them to me!"

Übung 92: Was gehört zusammen?

ÜBUNG 92 !

1. What's going on?
2. You had it all planned!
3. You did kill Sullivan's family!
4. It was all just a dirty trick!
5. All the evidence is in this room.
6. Why are you really here?

a) ☐ I have never killed anyone!
b) ☐ I'm here to destroy the evidence.
c) ☐ What makes you say that?
d) ☐ So give it to me!
e) ☐ You'll find out soon enough.
f) ☐ Of course I did.

“For the hundredth time, it’s over. Under Montgomery with protection money it was different. Now I’m doing it my way.”
“Then why do you still need the files? It was an accident. You were there yourself when Captain Montgomery gave me and Jordan the instructions. Mike Sullivan wanted to be transferred out of the unit. He didn’t want to be protecting illegal weapons transports at night and appear to be a loyal agent to his country during the day. He wanted out of Montgomery’s scheming wheelings and dealings. He had a little kid. He didn’t want to shoot. Do you think something like that is dismissed when someone burns down the place? Like you said afterwards, you cover the traces and make it look like you’re investigating. But it was clear from the beginning, that if anyone took notice of the facts, they could link everything together. And now this Hunter is digging everything up again.”
At these words Hunter smiled. His expression almost immediately twisted in pain as he felt that his other leg had started to fall asleep.

The moment was near. Soon he would intervene. He concentrated on the voices. He had to know exactly where the adversaries were standing. He could hardly see anything from his position.

ÜBUNG 93 !

Übung 93: Vervollständigen Sie die Sätze mit ***some*** *oder* ***any****!*

1. Miller doesn’t have/guilty feelings.

____

2. There wasn’t/light for Hunter to see by.

____

3. Hunter had barely/feeling in his leg.

4. Callaghan has/very hi-tech devices in her office.

5. We will have to call for/back-up soon.

6. Is there/way to save the situation now?

He held his breath once again. Callaghan was speaking appeasingly to Miller.

"I've already headed off this thing with Hunter. He's a complete idiot and apart from that, he's psychologically screwed. When he was in Italy, he fell in love with another agent and got his heart broken. Anyway, it doesn't matter. What I'd advise you to do, Stan, is to keep your trap shut. At the time, Montgomery had just flown out to the doomed operation in Milan and the transfers with the Russians and the Italians almost slipped through our fingers. If Lords Ashby and Snowdon hadn't reacted so quickly along with the Home Secretary, we would all have been lost along with Montgomery."

She paused at this point "Montgomery was my boss. I liked him. I was young. I learnt a lot from him. He liked you less, Stan. You were a shooting partner. You were always nervous. That I got the place in Montgomery's syndicate never surprised you. But what kind of complete idiot am I? I'd hardly climbed on to the boss's seat and you stepped into my previous position. You're trying to become the Captain of the most important unit using your old connections Stan Miller. Your boys should guide the weapons transport, nothing

more. And what did this make you do, you blockhead? In a blind panic, you send poor Sullivan, who was being kept in some outpost or other in his old age, to join his family in heaven."
Miller's rage could be heard in every syllable. "Callaghan, give me the transactions and the documents involved. You seized them when you cleared out Montgomery's office."

Her answer was cold. "You don't need the old documents any more. Do you want to destroy the ones where your name doesn't come up? You were in them Stan. Until today you were in them. But Auntie Helene took care of you. I'll bring Hunter back into line, Sullivan's murder won't come to anything. You should see that your boys toe the line. That they don't unintentionally meet impatient people with 'Macsters'.
Very easy, very simple. Early each morning you'll come to me and pick up your action plan for the next night. This week, two weapons deliveries are coming that we need to hide from the long arm of the law. One is just small things from the airport. The other tank sections will be delivered by shipping freight. Good night Stan."

ÜBUNG 94 !

Übung 94: Der Fall wird aufgeklärt! Bringen Sie die Sätze in die richtige Reihenfolge!

1. Service there throughout corruption was the Secret.

____

2. many been cover-ups there had.

____

3. involved Miller trading Montgomery and been in had arms.

---

4. family to quiet him Sullivan's been keep killed had.

---

5. cellar hidden files the in the were.

---

6. didn't scandal Callaghan huge want a public.

---

7. persistent in Percy investigations Hunter been their and had.

---

8. do them anything Miller stop would to.

---

9. continue arms to Callaghan the wanted illegal trading.

Miller's tone trembled as he replied bitterly, "Lick my arse. I'm going to do you in!"
A shot rang out.

Hunter wanted to spring up but his legs wouldn't hold him. They had gone lifeless from stooping behind the leather chair. More sounds cracked through the air. Someone, clearly a man, whimpered.

"Wait," Hunter told himself. "Wait till something else happens." He twisted his upper body back and forth and tried to find a better position in the tight space. A body lay folded up on the floor. Blood flowed over the floorboards. The whimpering grew louder.

A voice Hunter knew well panted, "I'm sorry, I wanted to do it. I only thought it would be better if I didn't wait for her orders. Then he really wanted to shoot her."

Percy's arrival must have confused the boss. The man with her was still silent. She got a hold of herself quickly and thanked the young agent for his quick-wittedness. She just wanted an explanation of the situation, when she became aware of the fact that he was wearing his 'mission suit'. He felt her gaze on his black suit and pulled off his hood with embarrassment. He brushed his tousled hair with his fingers.

"Oh," Callaghan's Shawn introduced himself, surprised. Then she and Percy turned towards Hunter. He held, it seemed to Percy, a dart in his hand. In the wall next to him was a small hole. The plaster was crumbling from it.

Hunter made use of the momentary confusion. He overcame the lameness in his legs. The agent jumped upright. At the same time he took his automatic pistol from the holster above his boots. He aimed at Callaghan.

On seeing the arrow, she quickly grabbed the waistband at the back of her skirt. She pulled out a small automatic pistol. She pointed the weapon in Hunter's direction with both hands.

Percy aimed his pistol alternately at the stranger with the arrow and his boss. Then he remembered the chapter from his textbook at the Academy. "Make a strategic decision when aiming. Keep all

threats covered." He decided on the man because until now no one was aiming at him.
But why was Hunter pointing his pistol at Callaghan? And why had Miller wanted to shoot her? Percy had definitely come too late.

Übung 95: Wie lautet die richtige Bedeutung der Idiome?

ÜBUNG 95 !

1. To jump out of your skin.
   a) ☐ to jump a long distance
   b) ☐ to be extremely startled

2. To be as white as a ghost.
   a) ☐ to be extremely pale
   b) ☐ to disappear suddenly

3. To give as good as you get.
   a) ☐ to attack back with the same force
   b) ☐ to give to people poorer than you

4. To beat someone at their own game.
   a) ☐ to outdo someone in an activity they are good at
   b) ☐ to beat someone by a very large margin

Hurried steps could be heard in the corridor. Around twenty men from the rapid response team ran into the room and secured the scene. Callaghan and Hunter immediately put their weapons away. Percy didn't have the same idea and was grabbed by two broad shouldered men in black combat suits. His spindly figure in the tight fitting 'mission suit' disappeared between the massive muscles of the other two, who had taken him from either side in a pincer movement. Only his head loomed above the men who were smaller than him.

"Thank you for dragging yourselves out," said Callaghan to the group. "I requested you several minutes ago."

"Sorry Ma'am," apologised the team leader. Almost tenderly, he stroked the badges on his uniform that showed his service level and said dryly:

"It's not actually our fault. It's happened quite often previously. Check the battery on your work mobile. When it's got enough juice, your emergency call may go through. But we can only track your current position with difficulty, because of the small voltage fluctuations. When they start we lose you permanently.

Callaghan didn't go any further. She righted her suit and checked the position of her hair. With a disparaging head movement, she motioned towards Miller who lay wounded on the floor, where he had been moaning unheard. Then Hunter saw the Captain had taken a shot to the thigh. With both hands he was trying to stop the bleeding. It foamed dark red between his fingers and some blood was seeping into the material of his trousers. The rest dripped on to the floor.

"Take him away and get hold of the Home Secretary," ordered Callaghan. To the two men who had Percy in custody, she said, "You can let Horn go. The guy saved my life with his brave intervention and knocked out Miller."

Percy was set free, receiving a few digs in the ribs on the way. The rapid response team left, shutting the door behind their leader.

Übung 96: Bilden Sie Konjunktivsätze in der Vergangenheitsform!

1. Miller shot Callaghan. Percy wasn't waiting in the corridor.

Miller would have shot Callaghan if Percy hadn't been waiting in the corridor.

2. Hunter defended Callaghan. His legs didn't fall asleep.

---

3. The rapid response team came earlier. Callaghan's phone was charged up.

---

4. Miller got away with it. He wasn't so arrogant.

---

5. Sullivan's family lived. Montgomery's career wasn't at stake.

Callaghan had identified him as her life-saver. What an honour! Percy beamed. What was up with Hunter? It wasn't just that his left sleeve was torn and bloody. Horn had never seen this ice-cold, penetrating stare with screwed up eyes. Hunter fixed his gaze on Callaghan.

"So no one will be arranging illegal weapons transportation in the next few nights," he began.

Callaghan attacked back, "Hunter, don't make too much of it. Your star is sinking. What you heard tonight is irrelevant."

"I wouldn't be so sure about that," he said.

"Oh really, my dear," she answered quietly. "You come in here dressed for a mission in the middle of the night. That isn't part of your job description in internal service. You've been caught in your superior's office. After that, what does your opinion count for?"

At this point in the discussion, Percy moved closer to the door. Hopefully Callaghan wouldn't notice that all these accusations applied to him too. She was focussing on Hunter.

"The diagnosis is extremely clear. You have been traumatised since Italy. Sound right? You can't forget this girl. Isn't that right? You hoped, in my office …"
Callaghan raised her pistol again slowly from where she'd put it behind her back when the rapid response team entered.
"That was your plan in Italy. Right? Gina died because of a corrupt, idiotic, unimportant conspiracy between the British Secret Service and the Italian weapons Mafia. Trapped between two sides, because she loved an agent."
"Because she knew too much, clever dick!" With that Callaghan threw a well-aimed kick at Hunter's wrist. His weapon slid away from him. He ignored the pain and immediately went into the defence position. Shawn wanted to intervene, but Callaghan waved him back, "Beat it!"

Kicking so high had made her skirt slide up around her hips. She didn't bother to right it. In nylon tights and pumps, she moved slowly to the side. Hunter moved with her. She left her defences open for a moment to stretch out both her arms and her tight jacket.
Hunter seized the moment. He rushed forward to place his palm under her unprotected chin. He paused halfway there.

ÜBUNG 97 !

Übung 97: Beantworten Sie die Fragen zum Text!

1. On what grounds does Callaghan want to fire Hunter?

____

2. Why is Percy confused by Hunter's expression?

____

3. Why did Gina die?

4. What was Callaghan planning to continue with Miller?

5. Why does Hunter have the chance to run at Callaghan?

The door was thrown open again, and the brisk tone of the rapid response team leader barked, "The Home Secretary for you Dr Callaghan. On line three."
As he spoke, the telephone on the desk had begun to ring.
Callaghan pulled down her skirt quickly. Then she picked up the receiver. The others stood undecided in the room.
"Hallo Wayne!" Callaghan greeted the caller, "Yes it's a terrible crime. Imagine, Stan Miller, 'wirepuller' in a weapons cartel. And it's been going on for years. Apparently under Montgomery, he was the star of the syndicate. I'm so disappointed in him."
After a short pause, she sighed into the receiver, "You're totally right. I'm far too soft as a boss. We'll make an example of this. Miller must be made to pay for his crooked ways. The reputation of the entire Secret Service is at stake if this goes public."
Finally she said, "Until tomorrow. Sorry again for disturbing you so late. Goodnight."
Strong tea with milk and lemon just like Hunter liked it. He nodded appreciatively at Percy who was just sitting down at the desk next to Hunter's with his own cup of freshly brewed tea.
"The youngster is moulting," thought the agent. Out loud he said, "Horn, that's what I call a decent cup of English tea." At the same time, he took a large slurp from the cup.

Übung 98: Finden Sie passende Synonyme!

"You can also have coffee if you (1. prefer) ____________________. I didn't know ..." As if he had uttered a threat, Percy was interrupted by his boss.

"No, no, the tea is (2. excellent) ____________________. What Englishman needs coffee?"

The other man's slightly confused, almost offended expression led Hunter to add hastily, "Of course I also like coffee. Yours isn't so bad, honestly."

There was a (3. gap) ____________________ in the conversation. Previously, they had been going back over the events of the previous evening. How should they

(4. proceed) ________________ now? Percy had suggested they should have a cup of tea first.

The junior agent stirred his tea fiercely with a metal spoon. The rhythmic clicking of the spoon against the edge of the mug seemed to inspire him. He put both hands around his mug and looked into the distance. He didn't seem to (5. be aware) ____________________ the narrowness of the room.

"What I heard from behind the leather chair isn't useful for us." Hunter postulated. "In a hearing, it would be our word against her's. As far as I see, thanks to her friends in the government and courts, Callaghan can claim what she wants. So we need written evidence." "We could (6. cite) ______________ Miller's files from the archive. We've also got Peterson's reports. Perhaps after all Miller's confessions …" Percy listed the evidence.

"And who would take the word of an agent who clearly covered up (7. weapons) ________________ transports for years? Who murdered? And against such a shrewd character as Callaghan? No, we need the relevant files from that time. Or the current contracts with the gunrunners. Miller wanted to look for both in Callaghan's office. He wanted to get a hold of both of them. He wanted to save his skin because we'd started to dig around." Hunter (8. paused) ____________________ for a moment and drank.

Percy carried on with the argument, "You were looking for that as well. And I showed up because I though if there was evidence then it was going to be in the lion's den. It seemed so banal to me to break into the office – if someone came, then I'd have to hide behind something."

"You're right," confirmed Hunter. "I'm a agent and pretty good at dealing with dangerous situations. Deductions and tracking I prefer to leave to the police. I don't have a sixth sense for it. But this time I tell you, Callaghan had the documents in her office. And I think I know where."

The ringing of the telephone interrupted their speculations. Percy zealously wanted to answer, but Hunter got there before him.

"I'll be there immediately," he said into the mouthpiece.
"Yes, I'll hurry," and "Goodbye."
Then he turned to his colleague, "Give me the spear, I'm going to the lion's den,"
"Good luck hunting," replied his colleague.

ÜBUNG 99 !

Übung 99: Welche Reaktionen rufen die folgenden Ereignisse bei den Personen hervor? Ordnen Sie zu!

1. Percy heard a sinister noise behind him in the cellar.
2. Hunter was moved to internal service.
3. Norma thought Callaghan was trying to do her job.
4. Percy appeared out of nowhere and shot Miller.

a) ☐ devastated
b) ☐ livid
c) ☐ stunned
d) ☐ petrified

It had been clear which direction the conversation would take. Callaghan was enthroned victoriously on her chair. Suit, hairstyle and make-up were perfect and showed no evidence of last night's incidents. She furrowed her brow and her eyebrows moved sadly upwards as she expressed her regrets to the agent.
What had happened yesterday was 'one of the blackest moments of her career', as she put it. She explained laboriously and at length how disappointed she was in Captain Montgomery. From the beginning of her career in one of the finest teams he had been her idol. She explained her suspicions at that time that Miller could have been involved and her helplessness as a young and inexperienced agent.

Hunter cursed the visitors' chairs in her office. He already was involuntarily leaning far back, his posterior hung just above the floor and his knees were sticking straight up. He tried to pull himself back out with both hands on the arms of the chair. Callaghan had reached the point in her story about the year of the events involving Montgomery and her mistrust of Miller the whole time up to the day of her promotion. First of all, she had been Captain Montgomery's successor when he was suspended. "So much for the poor inexperienced agent," thought Hunter – three years later head of the Secret Service.

Naively believing in the goodness of people, she had wanted to give Miller another chance and had promoted him to her old position as Captain of the 'Third Elite'. Here, Callaghan made a special effort to increase the melodrama of her performance. She sniffed quickly and was just wiping her nose with a tissue when she noticed Hunter's smug smile. The smile said to her, "I don't believe a word!"

Übung 100: Drücken Sie Ihre Überzeugung aus!
(to be convinced, to be sure, to know)

1. Everything will calm down now.

I'm sure everything will calm down now.

2. We can keep this between ourselves.

____

3. This doesn't need to get to the press.

____

4. You want to protect the reputation of the Secret Service.

5. You don't want to cause a scandal.

6. Miller will be adequately punished.

7. We never want this to happen again.

"What?" she reacted annoyed by his expression.

"Listen, just between the two of us. I know all about it. I heard enough last night from behind the chair," he explained calmly.

She started to object, but he was quicker, "And don't tell me about strategic questioning, that you were just pretending to be involved in weapons dealing to force a confession out of Miller."

He met her enraged snort with, "Such interview games would have been too ridiculous and undignified as well, Dr Callaghan. You're always in the picture here."

It was enough for him to argue from the depths of the seat. Now he sat on the edge with both hands resting on his thighs. Callaghan's features relaxed.

"You've got no chance whatsoever. You know that. My word against your's. You would need written proof."

As she said this, Hunter's gaze wandered to the Warhol picture above her head.

"You haven't got anything, because I don't give anything away."

This time the agent's sidelong glance remained longer on the picture before he turned back to her.
Callaghan's eyes narrowed and signalled to him that she understood what he meant. Her words confirmed the impression. "I could still suspend you today over psychological problems. Since Milan …"
This time she said no more.

Übung 101: Bedanken Sie sich bei Callaghan! Welche Formulierungen sind richtig?

1. ☐ I really appreciate this.
2. ☐ Thank you so much.
3. ☐ I'd rather not.
4. ☐ I won't let you down.
5. ☐ I wasn't expecting this at all.
6. ☐ Better not this time.
7. ☐ Never mind.
8. ☐ No, not at all.

"I know that since it happened sometimes I've been a bit distracted. What I've realised now is that Gina's death wasn't my fault. Why should I still blame myself? She said herself it was a put-up job. My love for Gina became a weapon for you Callaghan. A weapon against me. Please, call Norma and let her examine the depths of my psyche. Or do you just want to ignore the psychology department again Doctor?" As he was speaking, he apologised to Gina in this thoughts.
Callaghan was uneasy. Hunter noticed that her hands had closed on the back of the chair. Her knuckles were white.

Übung 102: Setzen Sie die Wörter an den richtigen Stellen ein! Diesmal sind es viele! Passen Sie also gut auf!
(soul, sniffing, tempting, tension, brusque, swore, pathetic, circles, trainee, nod, picture, glasses, frame)

"OK Hunter," she broke the 1. ____________ abruptly. "I won't do anything to you, you won't do anything to me. What do you think?"
Hunter hadn't been expecting this reaction. The situation was asking too much of him. The only thing that came to him spontaneously, that had been burning in his 2. ____________ for days, was "I want to return to external duties". He was annoyed with himself for the sudden tremor in his voice that made the words come out rather 3. ____________ and unmanly.
Her eyes blazed. "But of course if you want to. Then you'll be busy and won't think to come 4. ____________ around again."
She had regained her usual self-confidence. The agent felt humbled. He 5. ____________ to himself, "I'll get you. And I already know how."
Callaghan rose, "Hunter, we're going round in 6. ____________. Let's leave these things alone. You return to external duties. You're not the worst, you know."
Her proposition was 7. ____________ and she seemed to want to

be a little coquettish as she slowly changed legs and pushed a hip forward. She stayed in this position. "Perhaps I can offer you a position in the 'Third Elite'?"

The reply was 8. ______________, "No thanks, I'd like to go back to my old rapid response team."

Callaghan approved his choice with a majestic 9. ______________ of the head and added:

"Then you surely won't have a problem when, as an experienced agent, I place a young 10. ______________ in your care. Perhaps you'd like to give Horn the happy news yourself?"

She turned her shoulder and with two steps, was behind her chair. With her back to Hunter she busied herself with the Warhol picture and moved it back out of the way as the mechanism released one side of the 11. ______________ and it swung out of the way. Hunter stared in surprise. It clinked softly once, then again. Callaghan dug deeper into the wall behind the now folded 12. ______________. She turned back to him and waved two 13. ______________.

"Whiskey or Scotch? To great work together in the future!"

Abschlusstest

Übung 1: Bringen Sie den Dialog in eine sinnvolle Reihenfolge!

1. I'll just get her for you.
2. No, it's Jennifer.
3. Hi, is that Susan?
4. Cambridge 387512
5. Thanks very much.
6. Could I speak to Susan please?

Lösung: _ _ _ _ _ _

Übung 2: Welche Antwort ist richtig? Kreuzen Sie die korrekte Lösung an!

1. How do you do?

a) ☐ I'll show you.
b) ☐ Fine in this moment.
c) ☐ How do you do.

2. How is your new job?

a) ☐ It's very challenging.
b) ☐ It's in the centre of London.
c) ☐ I'm a senior manager.

3. Did you hear about Louise?

a) ☐ Yes, isn't it great?
b) ☐ I met her at a party.
c) ☐ I'm seeing her tomorrow.

Übung 3: Äußern Sie Ihre Wünsche!

1. (to get to know my new colleagues better)

____

2. (to have a well-earned rest)

____

3. (to make a good impression in my new job)

____

4. (to enjoy my birthday party without any stress)

____

Übung 4: Setzen Sie die richtige Präposition ein!

1. The off-licence closes ______ ten o'clock.
2. My birthday is ______ May.
3. I normally go to bed _______ midnight.
4. What do you do ______ Christmas Day?
5. I love the weather _____ the winter.

Übung 5: Was sagen Sie wann?

1. Congratulations!
2. What a nightmare!
3. Well done!
4. What a pity!
5. I'm really sorry.

a) ☐ My kitchen flooded at the weekend!

b) ☐ I passed my driving test!
c) ☐ My wife's just had a baby!
d) ☐ My cat was run over.
e) ☐ I didn't get the job.

Übung 6: Wählen Sie die höflichste Antwort!

1. Could you show me how to get to London Bridge?
a) ☐ It's over there.
b) ☐ Of course.
c) ☐ No, I don't know.

2. Do you know where the Royal Museum is?
a) ☐ I'm afraid I don't, sorry.
b) ☐ I'm not from here.
c) ☐ No, sorry.

3. Is there a chemist's near here?
a) ☐ No that I know of.
b) ☐ There's one just around the corner.
c) ☐ Round here, across the road.

Übung 7: Welche Antwort ist richtig?

1. Thanks for coming.
   a) ☐ No problem.
   b) ☐ Thanks for inviting us.

2. Would you like something to drink?
   a) ☐ That would be great, thanks.
   b) ☐ Yes, of course.

3. You've gone to so much trouble!

a) ☐ No trouble at all.

b) ☐ Of course I haven't.

Übung 8: Welche Wörter gehören zusammen?

1. back	a) ☐ round
2. to	b) ☐ forth
3. round	c) ☐ out
4. up	d) ☐ fro
5. in	e) ☐ down

Übung 9: Welche Wörter haben die gleiche Bedeutung?

1. Cheerio!
2. How are you?
3. Hi there!
4. Talk to you soon.

a) ☐ Hello!

b) ☐ We'll speak soon.

c) ☐ Goodbye!

d) ☐ How's it going?

Übung 10: Formulieren Sie vollständige Fragen!

1. (tell me newsagent near here)

Could you tell me if there is a newsagent near here?

2. (direct me nearest tube station)

____

3. (help me find National Museum)

____

4. (show me get to Oxford Circus)

____

5. (tell me where can find a cinema)

____

Übung 11: Um welches Kleidungsstück oder Material handelt es sich bei den Beschreibungen?

1. A smart, matching set of jacket and trousers or skirt:

____

2. Worn on the beach or at the swimming pool:

____

3. Protect the eyes from strong sunlight:

____

4. The end of a jacket or shirt sleeve:

____

5. Synonym for a dress:

____

Lösungen

Übung 1: 1. a 2. b 3. a 4. b 5. b 6. b
Übung 2: 1. strict 2. weak 3. bored 4. clearly 5. loudly 6. better
Übung 3: 1. was soaping 2. began 3. had been 4. had 5. came 6. had been ordered 7. had even had 8. had always come
Übung 4: 1. On the beach 2. Because she can't say three properly and her parents always correct her 3. Because Mike gets called away to work 4. She thought it would be thrilling, romantic, exciting and dangerous 5. Michelle splashes her with bath water
Übung 5: 1. wet 2. splash 3. moist 4. foam 5. bathtub 6. dry
Übung 6: 1. his 2. he 3. he 4. his 5. his 6. he 7. it 8. his
Übung 7: 1. suit 2. swimsuit/swimming costume 3. sunglasses 4. cuff 5. frock 6. cord 7. sleeve 8. lycra
Übung 8: 1. quieter 2. smarter 3. heavier 4. further 5. older 6. worse
Übung 9: 1. b 2. b 3. c 4. a
Übung 10: 1. ugly 2. bikini 3. laugh 4. leave 5. pavement 6. owner
Übung 11: 1. understood 2. wanted 3. had begun 4. had started 5. were 6. had handed 7. was 8. had been 9. had helped 10. had visited 11. gave 12. had almost broken
Übung 12: 1.a 2. b 3. b 4. a 5. b 6. b
Übung 13: 1. Newport, could you please go back to your office? 2. (Could you) sit down please. 3. Could you please shut the door. 4. Please stand up when I'm talking to you. 5. Please don't laugh. 6. Could you please eat your dinner.
Übung 14: 1. housewife 2. boss 3. secret agent 4. clerk
Übung 15: 1. A fifth 2. Three hundred and fortytwo pounds and ninety pence 3. The seventh of the first two thousand and four/the seventh of January two thousand and four 4. one meter seventy (centimetres) 5. ten thousand six hundred and seventy two 6. fifty cents/half a dollar
Übung 16: 1. a 2. b 3. a 4. a
Übung 17: 1. colossal 2. simultaneously 3. dragged 4. extremely 5. amused 6. cord 7. retro 8. heard
Übung 18: 1. b 2. f 3. c 4. a 5. d 6. e
Übung 19: sad, round, patterned, red-green, long, long, gangling, paternal, casual
Übung 20: 1. remains 2. sniffle 3. hesitate 4. stance 5. serious 6. dirty 7. pleasant 8. long
Übung 21: 1. He is Hunter's new assistant 2. A huge basil plant. 3. It falls out of the pot into Hunter's hands. 4. It's practical. They can eat it on sandwiches
Übung 22: 1. a 2. b 3. a

Übung 23: 1. worry 2. thin 3. elderly 4. noisy 5. difficult 6. little

Übung 24: 1. How was your evening out? 2. Did you enjoy yourself at the party? 3. What did you think of the music? 4. When did you get home? 5. Who did you see there? 6. Do you have to work today?

Übung 25: 1. Let's start work. 2. Let's have a cup of tea first. 3. Let's look at these files now. 4. Let's look at the documents very carefully.

Übung 26: 1. has not 2. does not 3. we will 4. let us 5. can not 6. we are

Übung 27: 1. a 2. b 3. b 4. a

Übung 28: 1. demoted 2. slowly 3. kind 4. important 5. rigid 6. passive

Übung 29: 1. What happened? 2. She was shot 3. Who by? 4. Someone broke in 5. That's terrible 6. I know 7. Did they catch him? 8. I don't think so

Übung 30: 1. could 2. putting 3. could 4. was bleeding 5. knew 6. turned 7. looked 8. had ripped

Übung 31: 1. Which 2. What 3. Who 4. Where 5. Why 6. How

Übung 32: let, was reserved, was regarded, could, say, had, met, didn't stand, entering, released, set, exploded, went, came, left

Übung 33: 1. devastating 2. standard 3. equipped 4. responsible 5. depot 6. respective 7. operation 8. termination

Übung 34: 1. culprit 2. mystery 3. suspiciously 4. undercover 5. plainclothes 6. conclusion

Übung 35: 1. squeak 2. creak 3. crash 4. bang 5. crack 6. splat

Übung 36: 1. The rat was kicked by Percy. 2. The cellar was lit by bright neon lights. 3. Numbers had been written on the boxes by the secretary. 4. The old cabinets were covered in dust. 5. The first file was picked up excitedly by Percy.

Übung 37: 1. unbelievably 2. previously 3. well 4. stylishly 5. hard 6. highly 7. impatiently 8. carefully 9. fast

Übung 38: 1. request 2. complain 3. trivial 4. disinterested 5. confused 6. ignore

Übung 39: 1. scent 2. shake 3. took 4. idiot 5. sack 6. pretend

Übung 40: 1. b 2. b 3. b

Übung 41: 1. for 2. in 3. through 4. at 5. from 6. above 7. with 8. by

Übung 42: 1. a 2. b 3. a 4. a

Übung 43: 1. foot 2. hand 3. knee 4. hand 5. fingers 6. elbow 7. head/forehead 8. hand

Übung 44: 1. a 2. b 3. b

Übung 45: 1. impatient 2. unimportant 3. illegal 4. inattention 5. irregular 6. unhappy 7. uncomfortable 8. non-violent

Übung 46: 1. gave 2. to look 3. tell 4. To begin with/At first 5. looked at 6. have the chance

Übung 47: 1. e 2. a 3. c 4. b 5. f 6. d

Übung 48: 1. b 2. a 3. a 4 b

Übung 49: 1. Percy is frequently doubtful about his ability as an agent. 2. Hunter often does things that confuse Percy. 3. Every day Hunter sits in his office and gets bored. 4. Today they found some new information on the case. 5. Soon after Percy went into the cellar he was attacked. 6. Hunter hardly ever drinks coffee in the morning.

Übung 50: 1. He has burnt his tongue biting into the first piece of macaroni. 2. Angrily he examined the clump of pasta with resounding name of 'Macaroni Sorpresa di Milano' and pushed his plate away. 3. He wanted to stay sober and clear-headed when he went through Miller's file. 4. Apart from that after a few days in the office he was already feeling the urge to do something active. 5. It was long past midnight when he finished studying. 6. It dealt with a case Hunter only vaguely remembered.

Übung 51: 1. investigation, investigator 2. suspect, suspicion 3. murder, murderer 4. perpetrator, perpetration 5. witness 6. police, policeman, policewoman

Übung 52: 1. Why don't you visit me at the weekend? 2. What about coming over for lunch? 3. Would you like to come to my birthday party? 4. How about going to the art gallery with me on Thursday? 5. What do you think of visiting the beach? 6. Do you want to see the new exhibition?

Übung 53: 1. see 2. write 3. eight 4. blew 5. knew 6. weak 7. peace 8. break

Übung 54: 1. for 2. on 3. in 4. down 5. forward 6. of

Übung 55: 1. traffic lights 2. seatbelt 3. brakes 4. North 5. map 6. limit

Übung 56: 1. a 2. b 3. a 4. b 5. a 6. b

Übung 57: 1. d 2. c 3. a 4. e 5. f 6. b

Übung 58: 2. I would like to have been better prepared. 3. I would like to know what happened 4. I would like to be able to help you. 5. I would like to get to the truth of the matter.

Übung 59: 1. We are conducting an investigation. 2. Do you know anything about the case? 3. Can you help us with our investigations? 4. We are looking for new information on the case. 5. We think you know what happened. 6. Do you have anything to add?

Übung 60: 1. c 2. b 3. f 4. a 5. e 6. d

Übung 61: made, heard, grabbed, rolled under, ducked down, crept along, glanced, changed, held, looked around, was covering, had vanished, thought, breathed in, sprang, swung, took in, led, stood, lay, crumpled up, was running, sticking, must have injured, followed

Übung 62: 1. d 2. b 3. e 4. a 5. f 6. c

Übung 63: 1. secret agents 2. a psychologist 3. Hunter's boss/Head of the Secret Service 4. elite agents 5. a policeman/secret agent

Übung 64: 1. b 2. e 3. c 4. f 5. a 6. d

Übung 65: 1. surgery 2. accuser 3. policeman 4. arrow

Übung 66: 1. Gina was wearing a nightdress which was very sexy. 2. Hunter was very happy that they had some time together. 3. She was an agent who had very special talents. 4. They were on a mission which was top secret. 5. Hunter was a man who liked to work hard and play hard. 6. It was very important that they solve the case soon.

Übung 67: 1. couldn't bear 2. jumped out 3. was able to stop 4. was 5. had started 6. holding 7. chewed 8. hadn't stopped

Übung 68: 1. No, I don't think Sullivan's family died by accident. 2. No, they don't have enough evidence yet to prove who killed Sullivan's family. 3. No, Hunter isn't finished as an active agent. 4. No, I don't think Callaghan is involved in the mystery. 5. No, Percy isn't useless as a secret agent.

Übung 69: 2. Could you clear up some confusion? 3. Could you help us with our enquiries? 4. Could you explain how events unfolded? 5. Could you tell us why you were there in the first place?

Übung 70: 1. a 2. b 3. b 4. b 5. a 6. a

Übung 71: 1. When 2. When 3. As 4. When 5. When

Übung 72: 2. They were an agent's wife and daughter, weren't they? 3. It seems a bit suspicious, doesn't it? 4. Something has been covered up, hasn't it? 5. It can be solved, can't it?

Übung 73: 1. I present to the court exhibit A. 2. I call witness number eight to the stand. 3. Do you swear to tell the whole truth? 4. Order in court! 5. Do you have any further questions?

Übung 74: 2. We already know a lot about what happened that night. 3. Callaghan is already getting suspicious. 4. Do you still want to get involved? 5. There's still a lot of work to do.

Übung 75: 1. b, g, h, k, n 2. a, d, f, j, o 3. c, e, i, l, m

Übung 76: 1. b 2. e 3. d 4. f 5. a 6. c

Übung 77: 1. Percy waited at the station for a long time. 2. They have been investigating the case since the beginning of the week. 3. Hunter hadn't eaten since breakfast. 4. The case had been allowed to lapse for several years. 5. Callaghan has been the boss for five days. 6. Montgomery has been retired since 1997.

Übung 78: 1. sure 2. silvery 3. possible 4. bags 5. grilling 6. drove 7. expectant 8. deciding
Übung 79: 2. When did you last see Mike Sullivan? 3. Were you present the night the witness died? 4. What were your movements on October 11th? 5. Do you have an alibi for the night of June 20th?
Übung 80: 1. Right now, Miller is trying to control himself. 2. Currently, Percy is watching the interview excitedly. 3. At this moment, Miller is beginning to sweat. 4. At the moment, Hunter is giving Miller a grilling. 5. Percy is learning a lot right now. 6. Hunter is currently feeling powerful.
Übung 81: 2. detective 3. administration 4. criminal 5. suspect 6. operation
Übung 82: 1. He's going to find the files on Miller. 2. He's going to get justice for Sullivan and his family. 3. He's going to expose Callaghan as a fraud. 4. He's going to restore his reputation as an agent. 5. He's going to make Percy admire him. 6. He's going to get back out of the office.
Übung 83: 1. b 2. d 3. a 4. c
Übung 84: 1. When 2. If 3. When 4. If 5. If
Übung 85: 1., 2., 5., 6., 7., 9., 10.
Übung 86: 1. d 2. c 3. a 4. e 5. b
Übung 87: 1. a 2. a 3. b 4. a
Übung 88: 1. the most 2. most trivial 3. fastest 4. most dangerous 5. tallest 6. fittest
Übung 89: 2. If Hunter had been better prepared, he would have brought his metal detector. 3. If Callaghan had had lots of defences, it would have been more difficult. 4. If he had known what he was looking for, he would have been more focussed. 5. If Percy had been less clumsy, he would have brought him too. 6. If he had had some concrete evidence, he wouldn't have needed to be here.
Übung 90: 1. was released 2. slid 3. sprang 4. was opened 5. take 6. heard 7. accompanying 8. to see
Übung 91: 1., 2., 4., 6.
Übung 92: 1. e 2. f 3. a 4. c 5. d 6. b
Übung 93: 1. any 2. any 3. any 4. some 5. some 6. any
Übung 94: 1. There was corruption throughout the Secret Service. 2. There had been many cover-ups. 3. Montgomery and Miller had been involved in arms trading. 4. Sullivan's family had been killed to keep him quiet. 5. The files were hidden in the cellar. 6. Callaghan didn't want a huge public scandal. 7. Hunter and Percy had been persistent in their investigations. 8. Miller would do anything to stop them. 9. Callaghan wanted to continue the illegal arms trading.
Übung 95: 1. b 2. a 3. a 4. a

Übung 96: 2. Hunter would have defended Callaghan if his legs hadn't fallen asleep. 3. The rapid response team would have come earlier if Callaghan's phone had been charged up. 4. Miller would have gotten away with it if he hadn't been so arrogant. 5. Sullivan's family would have lived if Montgomery's career hadn't been at stake.
Übung 97: 1. On psychological grounds 2. Because he is looking at Callaghan. 3. Because she was involved in a conspiracy and fell in love with a colleague. 4. Illegal arms trading. 5. Because she stops to stretch.
Übung 98: 1. would rather 2. wonderful 3. pause 4. carry on 5. notice 6. bring up 7. arms 8. stopped
Übung 99: 1. d, 2. a, 3. b, 4. c
Übung 100: 2. I'm convinced we can keep this between ourselves. 3. I'm convinced this doesn't need to get to the press. 4. I'm sure you want to protect the reputation of the Secret Service. 5. I'm sure you don't want to cause a scandal. 6. I know Miller will be adequately punished. 7. I know we never want this to happen again.
Übung 101: 1., 2., 4., 5.
Übung 102: 1. tension 2. soul 3. pathetic 4. sniffing 5. swore 6. circles 7. tempting 8. brusque 9. nod 10. trainee 11. frame 12. picture 13. glasses

Lösungen Abschlusstest

Übung 1: 4., 3., 2., 6., 1., 5.
Übung 2: 1. c 2. a 3. a
Übung 3: 1. I'd like to get to know my new colleagues better. 2. I'd like to have a well-earned rest. 3. I want to make a good impression in my new job. 4. I want to be able to enjoy my birthday party without any stress.
Übung 4: 1. at 2. in 3. at 4. on 5. in
Übung 5: 1.c 2. a 3. b 4. e 5. d
Übung 6: 1. b 2. a 3. b
Übung 7: 1. b 2. a 3. a
Übung 8: 1. b 2. d 3. a 4. e 5. c
Übung 9: 1. c 2. d 3. a 4. b
Übung 10: 2. Could you direct me to the nearest tube station? 3. Could you help me find the National Museum? 4. Could you show me how to get to Oxford Circus? 5. Could you tell me where I can find a cinema?
Übung 11: 1. suit 2. swimsuit/swimming costume 3. sunglasses 4. cuff 5. frock